THE FAUST CONSPIRACY

THE FAUST CONSPIRACY

James Baddock

Walker and Company
New York

To Melanie,
for putting up with it all.

Copyright © 1989 by James Baddock

Published in the United States of America in 1989
by Walker Publishing Company, Inc.

Library of Congress Cataloging-in-Publication Data

Baddock, James.
The Faust conspiracy / James Baddock.
p. cm.
Reprint. Originally published: Malvern, England : Malvern Pub.
Co., 1985.
ISBN 0-8027-1081-6
1. World War, 1939–1945—Fiction. I. Title.
PR6052.A3128F38 1989
823'.914—dc19 89-5512
CIP

Printed in the United States of America

10 9 8 7 6 5 4 3 2 1

PROLOGUE:
November 1942

"Fifteen minutes to go, Herr Vogel," shouted the pilot, above the din of the engines. Vogel nodded an acknowledgement and then turned to the man sitting opposite him, his back propped against the fuselage wall.

"Fifteen minutes," Vogel said in fluent, unaccented English.

"Right," said the other man, his Irish origins evident even in that one word. He did not look up from the revolver he was carefully checking. He seemed completely unconcerned by the prospect of being parachuted into the Irish Republic in the dead of night; whether this nonchalance was genuine or assumed was difficult to say but it showed that, at the very least, McConville had his nerves under control.

Which was just as well, in Vogel's eyes. He was going to have to rely on the Irishman a good deal over the next few days. Vogel's mission was to make contact with the Irish Republican Army and then to set up some sort of planned campaign in Ulster and on the British mainland; McConville was to set up the initial meetings. Privately, Vogel doubted if the mission would accomplish much. Since Dr. Hermann Goertz had been parachuted into Eire in 1940 there had been a string of unsuccessful attempts to use the IRA against the British, firstly through the Abwehr, then the SS. Virtually every German agent had been arrested by the Irish Security services within weeks of entering the Republic; Vogel had no desire to share their fate.

He hoped that this time would be different. McConville had been given an intensive training course at the spy school in Tegel and had proved his undercover skills; there should be

5

none of the amateurish mistakes that had wrecked the previous operations. If the IRA could be persuaded to mount an organised offensive of subversion and sabotage against the British then the risks would be more than justified. It would be a considerable feather in Vogel's cap . . .

He barely had time to grab a handhold when the pilot yanked the control column over in a desperate evasive manoeuvre. Above the clamour of the aero engines he heard the vicious stutter of machine gun fire. The Heinkel staggered in mid air as the tracers ripped through the fuselage.

The aircraft slewed crazily round and then straightened up. Vogel hauled himself to his feet and went forward into the cockpit. He tapped the pilot on the shoulder. "What the hell happened?"

"RAF fighter jumped us. He overshot, but he's still out there, somewhere."

"Where the hell are we? Are we over land?"

"No. Still over the Irish Sea."

"Fighter, port twenty!" yelled the front gunner.

The pilot reacted instantly; he pulled the column to port and then hauled it back. Vogel stared incredulously through the perspex screen at the fighter as it came straight at them, its guns spewing fire. The Heinkel lurched under an unseen hammerblow and the starboard engine erupted into flame. The aircraft's nose dipped violently and Vogel was thrown to one side as the plane began to spin.

The pilot wrenched at the control column, cursing; the spin slowed but they were still diving. "Help me!" he yelled. Vogel glanced once at the co-pilot, who was slumped lifeless in his seat, and then sprang forward. He grabbed the column and added his strength to that of the pilot. Slowly, the stick came back; just as slowly, the Heinkel's nose came up, until they were flying straight and level.

"It's all right," gasped the pilot. "I can hold her now. We'll have to crash-land. We're too low to bale out."

Vogel looked out of the cockpit screen and realised for the first time just how close the waves below were. Ahead was the darker smudge of land. "Can you reach the coast?"

"I'll try. Go back to the other passenger and get ready."

The pilot peered anxiously through the windshield at the line of cliffs hurtling towards them. They were too low . . . he needed height, for God's sake! With a strength born of desperation, he dragged the control column towards him. The Heinkel responded sluggishly, the port engine screaming in protest as he opened up the throttles. He had to have more speed . . .

Dear God, thought the pilot, we're not going to make it . . . And then the cliff-top flashed past, only feet below. With an involuntary cry of relief he throttled the engine back and brought the flaps right down, bracing himself for the impact . . .

The Heinkel slammed into the ground, reared up like a startled horse and then crashed back down. The starboard wing ploughed into a tree and was ripped off; the Heinkel slewed round and the port wing dug itself into the soft earth, snapping cleanly in two. The fuselage cartwheeled crazily across the ground, disintegrating with each impact, before finally skidding to a halt.

A shattering explosion ripped through the cockpit, as the fire from the engine reached the starboard fuel tank. The flames engulfed the pilot, before beginning to lick their way greedily along the shattered fuselage.

Vogel shook his head as consciousness returned; he had slammed into the airframe as the plane had careered across the field. The smell of burning brought his eyes flickering open; the sight of the flames only feet away galvanised him into action. Coughing as the smoke bit into his lungs, he clambered unsteadily to his feet and groped his way blindly towards the midships hatch. Someone was screaming, a shrill falsetto of terror and agony that went on and on . . . He turned around.

The pilot was still in his seat, trying frantically to release his safety harness; the entire upper half of his body was on fire . . . Deliberately, Vogel turned his back and reached for the restraining clip on the hatch. The damned thing was jammed! Dear God, no . . . Of all the deaths there could be, Vogel dreaded being burned alive the most . . . He slammed his shoulder against the hatch; it burst open and he tumbled out onto the wet grass below.

Still coughing uncontrollably, he began to crawl away from the blazing aircraft. Gradually, he found that he could breathe more easily and rose unsteadily to his feet, stumbling away for some yards before coming to an abrupt halt.

McConville was still in there.

The Irishman was his only means of linking up with the IRA. Without him, Vogel would be lucky to last five minutes . . . He swore, bitterly; there was nothing for it but to go back in and rescue McConville.

He took several deep breaths and then wrapped his scarf round his mouth. An image of the burning pilot slammed into his mind; Vogel pushed it aside and ran back towards the Heinkel, pulling himself up through the hatch. As he peered into the smoke-filled interior, he realised vaguely that the pilot had stopped screaming . . .

McConville was lying motionless, a few feet from the hatch. Vogel crouched down next to him, feeling for a pulse; it was irregular, but it was there. Vogel grabbed McConville under the armpits, dragged him to the hatch and rolled him unceremoniously through the opening, jumping down after him. Slinging the Irishman over his shoulder, he staggered away, swaying drunkenly, trying to force his leaden limbs into motion. He had to get clear . . .

With a deafening roar, the main fuel tanks exploded, throwing him forward. Covering his head with his hands, Vogel flattened himself to the ground, his eyes tightly shut. The debris pattered all around him; it seemed to go on and on. All he could do was lie there and try to keep the hellish images out of his mind . . . If any burning fuel spilled on to him, he would be a human torch . . .

After a few seconds, the rain of wreckage ceased; he opened his eyes and looked around him incredulously. Then, he crawled rapidly over to where McConville lay.

The Irishman was conscious, although blood was seeping from a wound just above the hairline. "Jesus!" he whispered, trying to focus his eyes on Vogel. "What the hell happened?"

"We crashed," Vogel said, simply.

McConville nodded and then winced. "And you pulled me out. I owe you for that." He looked up at Vogel, his eyes now more aware. "I always pay my debts."

8

"And I always collect. One way or another, I always collect," said Vogel, softly.

McConville shivered, involuntarily; Vogel was not the sort of man one would want to be indebted to. The debt would have to be repaid, one day; that much was certain.

And it would have to be repaid with interest.

CHAPTER 1

HERTFORDSHIRE, JULY, 1944

Charlie Lewis looked up at the sound of the aircraft, thinking that it was a bomber on a night exercise. It was rather earlier than usual, but Lewis did not attach any significance to the fact; there were more important things to consider, like catching that bloody poacher . . .

A glimpse of something moving out of the corner of his eye made him look up. To his amazement, he saw a parachutist descending, about a hundred feet up and fifty yards away. Lewis hesitated for a moment and then he began to make his way through the trees towards the spot where the parachutist would land, using all of his woodcraft and making no sound at all.

The sight of a shadowy figure in a clearing, twenty yards away, brought him to a halt. The parachutist was gathering in his 'chute, constantly looking around. To Lewis, the other man's actions seemed undeniably furtive; silently, Lewis unslung his shotgun and cocked it as he moved out of sight behind a tree.

The parachutist had finished hauling in his 'chute. As Lewis watched, he put his backpack down on the ground and took out a small shovel. He began to dig in the soft ground, still looking around every ten seconds or so.

That settled it as far as Lewis was concerned; the parachutist must be a German. Lewis had been invalided out of the Army after being wounded at Dunkirk, but the experience had done nothing to lessen his patriotism; he knew his duty.

With a feral grin of triumph, he stepped forward, the

shotgun cradled in his arms, aimed at the German. "Hands up!" he barked, realising that he sounded like a gangster in a second-rate film.

The parachutist spun round and then froze as he saw the shotgun. Slowly, he raised his arms above his head. Lewis felt a fierce surge of elation flood through him; he could already picture the reception he would be given when he took his prisoner into Markyate Police Station. He would be a hero . . .

Gesturing with the shotgun, he said, "Come on, Fritz. This way."

There was a movement behind him . . .

Vogel had seen that Roeder was in trouble with his 'chute, and kept a careful check on where the other man would probably land. But he could only watch Roeder for so long; the ground was now coming up to meet him. Vogel went into a landing crouch almost unconsciously; he had lost count of the number of parachute drops he had made over the years.

Bending his knees at the moment of impact, he rolled over once and came up onto his feet again, all in one fluid movement. He gathered in the 'chute with practised ease and then slipped off his backpack, using it to weigh down the bundled up canvas. Reaching into the pack, he took out a Walther pistol, checked the ammunition clip and then moved off.

At a rough guess, Roeder would probably be two hundred metres or so away, in the woods; Vogel hoped that he hadn't been injured in the landing. If he had, then the mission was over even before it had begun . . .

Vogel tensed as he heard Lewis' barked command and then moved stealthily in the direction of the sound. Within seconds, he had reached the edge of the clearing. "Bloody hell," he whispered under his breath; Roeder was standing as though transfixed with his hands raised above his head in an almost comical stance. There was nothing comical about the other man, however; by the way he was holding the shotgun he knew how to use it . . .

Vogel shook his head in disbelief. Roeder had allowed the

other man to take him completely by surprise . . . Vogel rapidly checked for signs of any other Britishers and then pocketed his gun; he would not need it. Instead, he took out a length of knotted cord, holding one end in each hand.

"Come on, Fritz. This way."

Vogel moved forward, holding the garrote in front of him. Lewis began to turn but Vogel sprang at him and looped the cord expertly over his victim's head, tightening it viciously so that it bit deeply into the flesh.

The shotgun fell to the ground as Lewis frantically tried to grab the cord to loosen its grip but it was embedded far too deeply for his fingers to grasp it. Blood was already oozing from Lewis' neck as the cord bit into it; panic-stricken, Lewis threw his body violently from side to side, his limbs flailing desperately, but Vogel held on, his features impassive as Lewis' face began to darken.

Aghast, Roeder watched the silent death-struggle; Lewis' eyes were bulging from their sockets and his tongue was protruding from his mouth in an obscene grimace. Lewis was on his knees now; Vogel was crouching over him, still holding the garrote tight around his throat. He yanked Lewis backwards and watched as the gamekeeper's heels drummed convulsively on the ground before they were finally still; despite this, he waited for another minute before unwinding the garrote from around the dead man's neck. Slowly, Vogel rose to his feet. Roeder was still staring down at the body, his face ashen; Vogel strode across the clearing towards him.

"What the hell were you doing letting him jump you like that?" Vogel demanded furiously.

Roeder could not seem to drag his eyes from the corpse. "You—You've killed him!" he gasped.

"What did you expect me to do? Offer him a drink?" snapped Vogel. "For God's sake, what were you doing, Roeder?"

At last, Roeder managed to look at him. "I—I didn't hear him."

"You didn't hear him," Vogel sneered. "You're an idiot, Roeder, and no mistake. Now the British are going to know we're here as soon as they find the body."

Not for the first time, Vogel cursed the fact that Roeder had been wished on him for this mission. Roeder had virtually no experience of undercover operations and had been given only the most basic training to compensate for this. Vogel had protested at the selection of such an amateur but had been over-ruled. It had been pointed out that Vogel himself had insisted that he needed an expert marksman who could speak fluent English; Roeder was the only candidate who fulfilled both requirements.

Vogel brought his temper under control; it was all in the past now and anger would serve no useful purpose. As a kind of therapy, he checked the shotgun; it had obviously been well looked after. The dead man must have been a gamekeeper, Vogel decided.

"Right, Roeder. We'd better get the body hidden away."

There was no reply. Vogel turned and saw that Roeder was once again staring down at the dead man in horrified fascination. "Oh, for God's sake, Roeder. You've seen dead men before, haven't you? Dammit, you've killed enough of them yourself!"

"Not—not like this," Roeder whispered.

No, not like this, Vogel realised with a flash of insight. Roeder had only seen his victims through a telescopic sight, not close up like this with the stench of death in the nostrils . . . This was what killing is really all about, Roeder my friend, Vogel thought, viciously . . . This was what separated the men from the boys.

He sighed in exasperation. "Take your chute, Roeder, and bury it at least a hundred metres from here. I'll deal with him." Acting like a bloody nursemaid, he thought, as he took hold of Lewis' ankles and dragged him away. But that was precisely his role, he reflected: to protect Roeder until he had got him into position so that he could squeeze the trigger.

And once that had been done, once the mission had been accomplished, Roeder would die.

Roeder looked at his watch for perhaps the third time in less than five minutes; Vogel noticed the action and resisted the impulse to check the time himself. They should have arrived in Euston at least ten minutes ago and the delay was obviously affecting Roeder's nerves. Vogel leaned back in his seat, the picture of unconcern, and looked out of the compartment window.

They had boarded the train at Hemel Hempstead at just before seven in the morning. The station had been deserted and so it was a reasonable bet that they would be remembered by the station staff, but there had been no alternative; Vogel wanted to get out of the vicinity of the killing as soon as possible. The body had been buried in a dense thicket and they had then hidden the parachutes some distance away, but it was only a matter of time before they were found. It all depended on when a search was instituted for the dead man . . .

Once that happened, the hunt would be on; at the very least, Vogel reasoned, it would be a murder investigation, even if the British did not suspect that the victim had been killed by German parachutists. The police would have virtually nothing to go on, however, and he and Roeder would be able to go to ground once they were in London; it would be like looking for a needle in a haystack.

What worried Vogel more was the suitcase that contained the equipment essential to the operation. They had two cases with them; one was innocuous, but the other, above Roeder's head, would sign their death warrants if the British were to search it. It would be impossible to explain away its contents; it had to be hidden as soon as possible.

Again, Roeder checked his watch; his nerves were clearly at breaking point. The sooner Roeder was safely under cover the better, Vogel decided. Roeder was proving to be just as great a liability as he had feared . . .

In spite of himself, Vogel let out a sigh of relief as the train pulled into the station. He nodded to Roeder and then stood up to lift down the suitcases, taking the incriminating one himself. Roeder opened the compartment door as the train slowed to a halt.

They approached the ticket barrier separately. Vogel looked casually around as Roeder handed over his ticket; the collector took it without even looking up. To Vogel's relief, Roeder walked away from the barrier at a normal pace.

Then it was Vogel's turn. He held out his ticket but avoided looking at the collector; he appeared to be searching for someone he was supposed to be meeting beyond the barrier. The collector took the ticket and Vogel walked on through, still looking around. Shaking his head, as if in disgust, he made his way to the Left Luggage Office.

Within a minute, he had locked the suitcase inside a locker. He tested the door to ensure that it was securely fastened and then pocketed the key, looking slowly round again, as though searching for the exit; in fact, he was checking to see if anyone had been observing him. Satisfied that nobody had been taking any undue interest, he walked unhurriedly out of the station.

Vogel could feel himself relaxing as he joined Roeder in the street outside. They were 'clean' now, carrying nothing that could arouse suspicion. When the time was right, he would return and remove the suitcase and its contents but, until then, it would be safe enough. The chances of that particular locker being searched in the foreseeable future were remote.

Roeder glanced interrogatively at a passing taxi; Vogel shook his head. They would get well clear of the station first; after that, they would simply disappear . . .

BERLIN.

The girl's face was plastered with make-up and she looked as though she hadn't had a decent meal for days; which was probably the case, Paul reflected, soberly. The effects of the Allied blockade were beginning to become very evident, particularly in the less salubrious areas of Berlin, where food of any description was generally only available on the Black Market at exorbitant prices. To eat, one needed money and in a lot of cases the only way a woman or a girl could eke out a living was to go on the streets.

Paul decided she was about fifteen, although, at first glance, she could pass for twenty or so; she was heading directly towards Paul, or rather towards the empty stool next to his at the bar. Her eyes were dull, listless, but when she spoke they adopted a pseudo-sensuous gaze, cultivated during an endless round of pick ups and rapid encounters.

"May I join you?" she asked, the practised note of invitation only too evident. Paul stared directly at her for several seconds, forcing her to look away, suddenly unsure of herself.

Paul reached into his pocket, took out his wallet and withdrew several banknotes before replacing it. He placed the notes on the bar-top between them but kept his hand pressed down on the money.,

"What's your name, fraülein?" he asked, gently.

"Trudi." The alluring expression had returned but she was unable to keep her eyes off the notes.

"Well, Trudi, I'd like you to do me a favour."

"Anything you like, Herr—?"

"Take this money and buy yourself a square meal, then go home and have a good night's sleep. By yourself. You could do with it, I think."

The girl looked confused. "But—what do I have to do for it?"

"Nothing. Nothing at all. Just take a night off, understand?"

"And you're giving me money just to do that?" she asked disbelievingly.

"Yes. Go on, take it." She snatched up the notes, perhaps afraid he would change his mind.

"Thank you, Herr—?" Again, she paused, waiting for him to give his name but this time there was no contrived tone of voice, just a fifteen year old girl who had been given a present and didn't know how to say thank you.

"Never mind that. Just do what I said."

"Thank you, mein Herr. I'll do as you say, I promise! Thank you!" The girl hurried out of the bar, leaving Paul shaking his head at his own quixotic gesture.

The barman came over as soon as Paul was alone. "Herr Koenig?"

"Yes?" Paul replied.

"Fraülein Hoffmann is upstairs, if you'd like to visit her?"

Paul smothered a grin. "Is she? Which room?"

"The usual one, Herr Koenig."

Admiral Wilhelm Canaris took a sip of schnapps and looked at the man sitting in the threadbare armchair opposite him. Paul Koenig was tall and blond-haired, with the Nordic good looks one saw on the SS recruiting posters; as Canaris well knew, Paul was as likely to pose for such a poster as Hitler was to change his name to Meyer. He gave the impression of being a nonchalant man-about-town but the blue eyes, older than his thirty years, gave the lie to that image. Paul was tough and, where necessary, ruthless. When Canaris had been head of the Abwehr, the German Military Intelligence organisation, he had regarded Paul as being his top undercover agent; Paul would need all of his resources for the mission Canaris had in mind . . .

"I've asked you here, Paul, for a very specific reason, as I'm sure you realise."

Paul nodded. "Is this room secure?"

"Absolutely." Canaris smiled, briefly. "I can guarantee it."

"Fair enough. So what do you want me for, Admiral? Is it linked with 'Valkyrie'?"

"Quite intimately, I'm afraid." Canaris took a further sip from his drink. "We have received details of an SS operation codenamed 'Faust'. And it's just as well we did. It could be catastrophic for us."

"Why?"

"Because, according to our sources, it's an assassination mission. 'Faust' is also the codename they have given the target."

"Who is it?"

"We don't know. It must be someone at or very near the top. Our sources can't discover who and that convinces me we must stop them."

Paul stared incredulously at Canaris for several seconds without speaking.

17

"Why the hell are they trying a stunt like this; now of all times?"

"Who knows? It's probably one of their death-or-glory stunts, cooked up by Skorzeny—he's mad enough to do anything these days. It may even have been put together to wreck our own plans. Whatever the reason, if they are successful then we can forget about 'Valkyrie'—von Stauffenberg's bomb, everything."

"You're certain of this?"

"As certain as we can be. The SS are sending two men to England. One of them is Karl Vogel. You may have heard of him."

Paul nodded. "One of their best undercover agents."

"Exactly. The other is a man called Roeder. He is a top marksman. He won shooting prizes in the Army before the war and is now used as an assassin, so it doesn't really leave much doubt, does it?"

"I accept that," replied Paul. "But do you really have no idea who 'Faust' is?"

"It has to be a fairly important target or they wouldn't be sending someone like Vogel to England. So it has to be Churchill or perhaps Eisenhower, Montgomery or Patton."

"So you want this operation stopped," said Paul, flatly.

"Yes," said Canaris, slowly. "But there is a problem. They are already in England. They were parachuted in last night."

Paul stared at the other man. "Then what do you expect me to do? Wave a magic wand?" He paused and then continued, quietly, "I would have thought your next move was obvious, anyway."

"Really?" asked Canaris, coldly.

"Really. There's only one thing you can do, tip the British off." He glared defiantly at Canaris. "It's the only way, sir."

"Betray them, you mean," said Canaris, flatly. "They are Germans, after all."

"If that's the way you want to look at it, then yes. But if you want to save 'Valkyrie', then it'll have to be done."

Canaris nodded slowly to himself. Yes, he had been right; Koenig was just as cold-bloodedly professional as he had remembered. He had come to the right man. "We have already considered this option. Unfortunately, we have very little information we can give them. We do not even know who 'Faust' is, not for certain."

"Better than nothing, however."

"It would be, if it was our only course of action. There is, however, an alternative."

"Which is?" Paul's voice had suddenly gone very cold, as if he knew what Canaris was about to say.

"We could send in a team of agents to track them down."

"You what?" Paul gasped incredulously. He stared at Canaris. "In England? What chance would they have? It's a suicide mission. Anyway, how would they do any better than MI5? They'd have no more to go on."

"Well, they would, actually. We've got our source at SS HQ to keep us informed. As soon as we receive any news, it will be passed on immediately."

"What news? If they've got any sense, they'll go to ground. No signals, no communication, nothing. That's what I'd do, in their position."

"Exactly. You understand how to survive and operate behind enemy lines. You know the procedures.

"You want me to lead this group, then." Paul's voice carried no inflection of tone; it was as though he'd expected it all along.

"Yes," said Canaris, slowly. "You've had experience behind enemy lines, you're resourceful and capable, you speak English fluently—in fact, you lived there for five years before the War. You are far and away the best man for the job."

"Spare me the flattery and find someone else. This is a suicide mission. The British Security forces are too damned good; you know that as well as I do. A penetration operation like this would take weeks, months, to set up and even then the odds would be stacked against it. How many agents have we managed to infiltrate successfully into Britain since 1939? The group would be caught, probably long before it got anywhere near Vogel and Roeder. As I said, find someone else."

"There is no-one else. Koenig, this is absolutely vital."

"Why? Why is it so vital that you want to send in a squad to find this 'Faust' group, when they haven't the slightest chance of finding them and are almost certain to end up in front of a firing squad? 'Faust' isn't THAT important—"

"Consider it a direct order, Koenig." Canaris' voice was icy with authority.

"I don't care what you call it—I'm still not doing it."

Canaris said nothing for several seconds. He seemed to be making a great effort to control himself and, when he finally spoke, it was with barely subdued rage. "In a few weeks' time, Koenig, as you know, Operation 'Valkyrie' will be put into motion. Adolf Hitler will be killed and his lackeys overthrown. There will be a new government, the SS thugs will be swept aside and we will begin peace negotiations to save Germany. Surely you do not wish to jeopardise all this?"

"I can do without the propaganda, thank you. Just tell me what difference my not going to England will make."

"One of our main aims is to negotiate an honourable peace with Britain and the United States—"

"I know all this—" interrupted Paul.

"I am reminding you, so that you will know exactly what is at stake. An honourable peace with the Western Allies and a pledge to allow us to go on fighting the Russians, our true enemies. Maybe even to join forces with Britain and America against the Bolsheviks but, at any rate, peace. Eliminate Hitler and the Nazis, and then negotiate. You know all this."

"Vividly."

"Then consider how the British would react if Churchill, for example, were to be assassinated by SS fanatics. Would they be very willing to negotiate peace terms with us after that? Or the Americans, if Eisenhower or Patton were to be killed?"

"They'd be furious at first but if they were really interested in a negotiated peace, they'd still sit down and talk. In fact, removing someone like Churchill, if it is him, might even help us—his successor might be less set on unconditional surrender. No, I don't think it would make any difference. I don't think they'll be willing to negotiate anyway, not now they're in France. Why should they? A year at the most and they'll be here. Why settle for less?"

"If you believe that they will not negotiate with us, why are you working for us? Our entire raison d'être is based on that premise—an honourable peace."

"There are other reasons for opposing the Nazis than the hope that we won't get beaten so badly—I notice that we weren't very active when Germany was winning but, now we're losing, Hitler's suddenly the villain of the piece, not the demi-god we made him out to be. Let's be honest, a lot of us are looking to save our own skins.

"I think Hitler ought to be opposed, simply because his is an oppressive, evil regime. For our own sakes, so that we can live with ourselves afterwards, we must oppose him, not because it might make the Allies more favourably disposed towards us, but because he's an evil bastard who deserves to die. Slowly. What the Allies do, or don't do, is irrelevant. I oppose Hitler because of what he stands for, not because the Allies might let us off lightly."

Canaris was taken aback by Paul's uncharacteristic vehemence, but he persisted. "Then help us fight him, by finding and stopping this operation."

"I've told you. I don't think it'll make any difference to us whether it succeeds or not."

"Our commanders do not agree with you."

"That's their problem. They're not being asked to carry out a suicide mission, are they? If they think it's that vital, let them find these killers." Paul's anger was evident; he was being manoeuvred into a corner and he knew it.

"Look," said Canaris, trying to make his voice sound as reasonable as he could, "We will give you all the support we can muster. You will be able to choose your own personnel. In fact, you can have Anton Lorenz—the two of you make a good team. We will give you the telephone number of our radio contact in London. You will be able to communicate with him by telephone at any time of the day or night. He will have no idea of your identity or location, but you will have instant access to him. He'll be able to pass any messages on to me within twelve hours; and you will have a reply within

21

twenty-four. You will have the best papers the Abwehr Forgery Section can produce—and you know they are always damned good. Also, you will have access to 'Jaguar', our top intelligence source in London, a man who will be in an excellent position to help you track down Vogel and Roeder. In short, you will be given every back-up and assistance that you will require."

Paul shook his head. "No. It's still a suicide mission."

Canaris sighed and reached into a briefcase. He had not wanted to do this, but Paul had left him no choice. He passed a sheet of paper over to Paul; it was a photocopy. "Read that, Koenig. Especially the name at the bottom."

Paul took the paper from him and read it; as Canaris watched, he saw Paul's expressicn change. His eyes were glacial and seemd to be looking at something that was a long way away, both in space and time.

"I'll do it," said Paul. There was a harsh edge to his voice. "I'll get Vogel for you, Admiral. And when I find him, I'll kill the bastard."

HERTFORDSHIRE.

Police Sergeant Fraser was cursing as he followed Bill Webster into the copse; he was soaked to the skin. The rain had started as soon as they had left Markyate Police Station and was now a torrential downpour. He let out a voluble oath as he stumbled over a root and then glared round at the young constable behind him, as if daring him to make any comment. But PC Leeson seemed preoccupied as he trudged along behind, carrying a shovel in each hand. As well he might be, thought Fraser as he turned back to follow Webster. Leeson was probably not relishing the next few minutes; nor, for that matter, was Fraser.

Webster came to an abrupt halt. " Here it is," he said pointing down at a shallow hole in the sodden earth. He moved away as Fraser approached and looked down into the hole.

For a moment he did not recognise the mud-soaked object in the pool of water that was gathering at the bottom of the hole but then, with painful suddenness, it was only too obvious that it was a human foot. The shoe and part of the ankle were visible but the rest of the body was buried.

"It was the dog that found it," Webster said nervously. "Out for the morning walk—she got a scent of something and dived off into the woods. By the time I caught up with her, she'd dug this hole."

Fraser nodded, only half listening, Webster had told them all this when he had come dashing into the station and was probably only talking to distract himself from what he had found; Fraser could sympathise with him.

"Right, Mr. Webster. We'll see to it now, if you don't mind."

"Thanks."Webster forced a wan smile. "You'd think I was used to dead men by now, after two years in the trenches but it was a hell of a shock, I can tell you."

Fraser waited until Webster had disappeared before he took one of the shovels from Leeson. Silently, the two policemen began to dig.

Fraser had guessed who it was, even before they uncovered the face; only Charlie Lewis wore green corduroy trousers like that. Out looking for poachers, thought Fraser. Only this time, he had been the victim....

The body was lying face upwards; Fraser put aside his shovel and bent down. He pushed the mud carefully away from the face. He heard a stifled cry from Leeson behind him and fought down the bile rising in his throat as he saw the bulging eyes and protruding tongue. There was no real doubt; Lewis had been strangled. He stood up and turned to face Leeson, grateful for the opportunity to look away.

"You all right, son?"

Leeson nodded; his face was ashen but he was doing his best to control himself. Fraser nodded in approval. "Right, son. Get back to the station and get on the blower. Tell County HQ that we've got a murder on our hands. Tell Alice to round up Jack and Wilf—I know they're off duty, but I need them. Then get back here. Got that?"

"Y—yes, Sarge," Leeson stammered.

"Good lad. Now get moving."

Fraser watched Leeson leave and then looked down at the body. So this is it, he told himself; your very first murder enquiry. There was no immediately apparent motive; Lewis had been very popular with the locals. Whoever killed him must have been foolhardy, thought Fraser; Lewis never went out on any of his nocturnal patrols without his shotgun.

Which was nowhere to be seen, he realised belatedly. Had the killer taken it? Fraser did not like that thought at all.

But why here? he asked himself. The killer must have stalked Lewis, must have taken him by surprise and yet, as Fraser well knew, Lewis was an expert woodsman. And then there was the method; strangulation. Fraser frowned. The killer would have had to be as good as Lewis in the woods and then to be both strong and vicious enough to overpower and strangle an armed man; Lewis had been no weakling, even with his wound.

It was then that he remembered being awoken from his sleep on Friday night by the sound of an aircraft. He was a light sleeper and had grown used to being disturbed by the RAF night exercises, but this had been a solitary plane which had been much earlier than usual....

Fraser felt a chill of foreboding. It looked as though this was going to go a lot higher than the County Police.

CHAPTER 2

HAMBURG, GERMANY.

"What is your name?"

  "Antony Lawrence."

  "Date of birth?"

  "7th August, 1913."

  "Place of birth?"

  "Hounslow, Middlesex."

  "Parents' names?"

  "John Peter Lawrence and Edith Masters."

  "Where did they come from?"

  "Both from Hounslow. They were married on June 12th, 1910."

  "Where are they now?"

  "Both dead. Killed during the Blitz."

  "What's your sister's name?"

  "I have no sisters. I am an only child."

  "What do you do for a living?"

  "Brush salesman."

Paul sat back and nodded. He spoke German, for the first time; the entire "interrogation" had been conducted in English. "Very well, Anton. That will do."

Anton Lorenz frowned. "I beg your pardon?" he asked, in fluent, unaccented English.

Paul chuckled. "Well done, Anton," he replied in English. "You're word perfect on your cover."

"I should be," said Anton sourly. "There isn't exactly a lot to it, is there?"

"I know," Paul agreed. "But there hasn't been time to set up anything more substantial. We'll just have to make do."

"It won't be the first time, eh, Paul?" Anton grinned.

"It certainly won't, Anton. Anyway, let's take a closer look at our quarry." He passed over a folder. "There's a detailed dossier on him in there, but I'll give you the bare outlines now."

Anton nodded; he made no move to open the folder.

"SS—Sturmbannfuehrer Karl Vogel," Paul began. He did not refer to any notes; clearly he knew Vogel's dossier by heart. "Born in Berlin in 1911. His father was killed at the Somme in 1916. His mother found herself destitute after the war, what with rocketing inflation and no steady income, so she turned to prostitution. Vogel grew up with that knowledge and, when he could not get any work himself in the late Twenties, he became very embittered. He was a ripe candidate for the Nazi Party and they recruited him in 1929.

"Now we come to a crucial part in his development. He came home one night in 1930 to find that his mother had been strangled by one of her customers. Vogel managed to find out who had done it, but, instead of reporting it to the police, he went round to the murderer and took his revenge. It was— well—messy. Vogel apparently went berserk; there wasn't much left of the other man by the time he finished. He was arrested but never charged; his release was engineered by none other than Reinhard Heydrich himself, who immediately adopted Vogel as his protégé.

"From then on, it was roses all the way for Vogel. He joined the SS and rose rapidly through the ranks. He was probably involved in the murder of Ernst Roehm during the 'Night of The Long Knives' in 1934."

"The SA leader?" said Anton, impressed.

"The very same. Vogel was then trained in undercover work as well as in both armed and unarmed combat. He learned English and was sent to England in 1936 for three years. By the time he returned to Germany he could pass as an Englishman. Since then, he's been involved in at least four missions abroad—Belgium 1940, Egypt 1941, Eire 1942, and North Africa in '42 and '43. So he's had plenty of experience in undercover operations; he's regarded as the best agent the SS have."

"He sounds it."

"He's a professional, Anton, make no mistake about it. There's none of the SS fanaticism about him. He plans everything down to the last detail, but he's got enough flexibility to change his plans at the last minute if he has to. He's calculating and ruthless; if he has to kill someone, he does, but there's no evidence to show that he enjoys doing it. There's been no repetition of that berserker rage when he took his revenge on his mother's killer, so don't expect him to lose control under pressure, because he won't."

"No weaknesses?"

"No known ones, no. He doesn't smoke, drinks only sparingly and keeps his relationships with women on a very casual basis. There isn't even a slavish devotion to Hitler that could be exploited."

"Why does he do it then? Risk his life behind enemy lines?"

"Nobody really knows. It may be that he has to prove something to himself, or it might be pride; apparently, modesty is not one of his virtues. Could be arrogance; he's the best there is and he's damned well going to prove it. But that's only a guess. Whatever his motives are, the fact remains that he's damned good. And it's up to us to track him down."

"A tough one, Paul."

"Amen to that," said Paul softly, almost to himself. "But we've got to find him.... We must."

HERTFORDSHIRE.

Fraser watched the other man closely. He was over six feet tall and broad, with dark hair and blue eyes. His name was Tyler. He walked with a very slight limp that favoured his left leg; despite this, Fraser decided that he'd rather not get involved in a fight with him. Tyler had arrived that morning from London, with a second man whom he had introduced as Randall. They carried cards that said they were in Special

Branch, but Fraser doubted that. They didn't look like policemen. More like MI5. Fraser's premonitions about Lewis were coming true, and very rapidly; it was less than twenty-four hours since Fraser had uncovered the body, yet Tyler had already taken over the police station. At this moment, he was sitting behind the rickety desk that had been Fraser's personal domain for the last five years; such was the unconscious authority of the man that Fraser had not even thought about protesting. Nor had Detective Inspector Hart, the fourth man in the cramped office; but then, he wouldn't, thought Fraser sourly. Hart was far too interested in furthering his own career, and any indignation he might have felt at having the investigation taken over by Tyler had been carefully concealed. Tyler was London, as far as Hart was concerned, and London meant promotion. Hart would bend over backwards to help, while carefully arranging that he gained the kudos.

Tyler put down the forensic report, and nodded approvingly over at Fraser. "You were right, Sergeant. It does look like a trained killer. The report mentions that the marks on the neck were probably caused by a garrotte."

"Well, he was obviously strangled," said Hart, with uncharacteristic lack of forethought. "It was almost certain to be by a rope."

"A garrotte is more than just a length of rope," explained Tyler, mildly. "It's a killer's weapon, knotted in just the right places for maximum effect on the windpipe. Precisely the sort of thing a trained killer would use—our own commandos use them."

Now how would you know that? Fraser wondered, but said nothing. Although it might explain the limp . . .

"Right," said Tyler, briskly. "I want a complete search of the area where Lewis was found. The whole works, dogs, the lot. Tell your men to look for any signs of anything being recently buried, Inspector. I've asked the Army to lend them some of their mine detecting equipment, so if there's anything metallic buried, they'll find it. I also want house to house enquiries. Lewis was last seen—when?—Friday night. That means we have a period of over forty-eight hours to cover. I want to know if anyone saw Lewis during that time, or if they noticed anything unusual—any strangers, that sort of thing. Or if they heard anything suspicious, anything at all— especially that aircraft you heard on Friday night, Sergeant."

"So it was a German plane?" asked Hart.

"Well, we checked with the RAF and the Yanks, and it wasn't one of theirs, so draw your own conclusions, Inspector. Right, next thing. I want the staff at all the local railway stations interviewed, see if they remember anyone boarding a train early on Saturday morning or Sunday morning. Also anybody out of the ordinary on Monday morning, but I think that's less likely—the post-mortem examination reckoned he was killed either on Friday or Saturday; I can't see them hanging around until Monday."

Fraser coughed, apologetically. "We've already taken statements from the railway staff. We've got a number of descriptions of various 'strangers', but none of them are very helpful. They could fit almost anyone. Anyway, we don't know how many we're looking for. Or even if they're all men." He caught the look of surprise on Hart's face; clearly, that last thought had not occurred to him.

"Good. Well done, Sergeant," said Tyler, smiling faintly. "I'm beginning to think my presence here is superfluous." The smile faded. "However, we have to face up to certain facts. The killer is almost certainly miles away by now, and we have precious little to go on. We need every scrap of information we can lay our hands on, and we need it quickly. We must prevent whatever that killer's come here to do."

He paused, and then continued, "And we may not have much time."

KILBURN, LONDON.

Vogel checked his watch as he entered the pub; it was exactly eight o'clock. The bar was filled with cigarette smoke, but he recognised McConville instantly, standing at the bar, drinking a pint of beer. Pushing his way through the crowded customers, he went up to the other man.

"Evening," he said.

McConville glanced at him, and relaxed, imperceptibly. "Evening," he replied. "What'll you have?"

"A pint," said Vogel. "Bitter."

McConville called the barmaid over. "Two pints of your excellent bitter, me darlin'." His Irish accent had become much more pronounced. Vogel smiled to himself— McConville seemed to be deliberately living up to the popular image of the "bog" Irishman.

"How are things?" asked the Irishman.

"Fine. Couldn't be better." Which meant no, I haven't been followed here. "How about you?"

"Top of the world." Which meant that he was clean, too. "I must say, it's rather a surprise to see you. It's been a long time."

"Eighteen months," agreed Vogel, sipping his beer.

"What have you been doing with yourself?"

"Oh, this and that. Here and there."

"Would you like a seat? There's a table over in the corner."

"Yes, alright."

When they had sat down, McConville lowered his voice. "Well, what do I call you?"

"Kenneth Vernon. You?"

"I'm still McConville."

"Good." Their voices were low, but not noticeably so. Every now and again, Vogel's eyes wandered to the barmaid or over to an attractive girl at the table next to theirs, sitting with what appeared to be a family group. To any observer, they were two reasonably young men eyeing up the possibly available young women.

"What can I do for you, then?" asked McConville.

"I want a girl, Sean."

"Don't we all," McConville chuckled. "That barmaid would probably be willing, but somehow I don't think that's what you had in mind."

"No, not exactly. She would have to be very attractive, sexually experienced, and able to obey orders, without question."

"I'd like one like that myself," observed McConville. "You're not thinking of using her as a Mata Hari?"

"I'm not that naive. She would have to sleep with someone she might not find very attractive. She would therefore have to be a convincing actress. I would also want photographic equipment—camera, film and developing apparatus."

"I see. Blackmail. I can think of one or two women who'd fit the bill. One, in particular, but she'd only do it for the Cause. She's even more fanatical than I am."

"Would she do it if you ordered her to?"

"Yes."

"If I ordered her to?"

"If I told her to obey your orders, yes."

"Would she ask awkward questions?"

"Not if I warned her off."

"Can you get hold of her within the next few days?"

McConville nodded. "Certainly. I don't suppose you'd like to tell me why you want her?"

"I've told you. I want her to seduce somebody."

"So you don't want me to know. Fair enough. One thing I will need to know, though. Will whatever you're doing interfere with any IRA activities?"

Vogel shook his head. "Not in any way."'

"That's a relief." McConville was in charge of a network of a dozen or so IRA members in London, and was also in touch with two other units in south-East England; one of their main methods of communication was the Personal Columns of "The Times", where apparently innocuous advertisements would contain coded messages or instructions. This was how tonight's meeting had been arranged; that night in the Irish Republic when the 'debt' was incurred, McConville and Vogel had decided on a simple message that Vogel could place in the column if he ever needed the Irishman's help. The rendezvous arrangement was simple: two days after the advertisement appeared, McConville would be in the White Horse pub in Kilburn at eight o'clock in the evening. If either man had been unable to make the rendezvous, then there would have been a fallback meeting arranged for forty-eight hours later. It was a watertight system—nobody else knew of it, and so there was no chance of it being "blown".

"When do you want to meet the girl?" asked McConville. "Or don't you?"

"Oh, I'll have to," said Vogel. "When can you get hold of her?"

"Two days?"

"Thursday night, then?"

"Should be all right, yes."

"Where?"

"Not here. Or my local. Do you know the Railway Tavern, in Hampstead?"

"I can find it."

"Same time?"

"Say 8.45."

"Right. I think you'll find she's suitable."

SUFFOLK COAST.

John Gilmore often walked along the beach on his way home from Jean Matthews' cottage. It was not the most direct route to his own house but he liked to wander across the dunes and along the shore. It also kept him away from any prying eyes that might notice his regular nocturnal visits to Jean Matthews' cottage.

A movement out at sea, half-sensed, half-seen, brought him to a halt. With incredulous eyes, he watched the unmistakeable silhouette of a submarine come into view out of the darkness. Concealing himself behind a dune, he watched the approach of the dinghy. The two men waded silently ashore and then moved soundlessly into the dunes. Equally silently, or so he thought, Gilmore followed them. These were German spies—that was a certainty. It was his duty to follow them and see where they went.

He ignored the cautioning voice in his head that told him to let them go, to head back to Jean's and use her 'phone to alert the police. First, he had to find out where they were going or, at least, he had to be able to give clear physical descriptions. Gilmore was certainly no coward.

The German agents paused for a full two minutes, as if waiting for something. Then, one of them rose to his feet and moved off into the shadows to the right. The other moved off to the left. Gilmore realised what had happened—they had heard him and were looking for him. For the first time, he fully realised his own danger. There could be no doubt what would happen to him if they found him.

Carefully, he eased himself backwards, trying to make no sound. Crouching low, he crept through the dunes, heading back towards the beach, although he had no intention of exposing himself on the shore itself. Gilmore intended to make his way through the dunes, which he knew like the back of his hand, and head towards Jean's cottage.

Every sound, no matter how small it was, made him wince; there was no way of knowing how near the others were. Every few moments, he stopped and listened, his ears straining to catch the slightest noise that might give an indication of his pursuers. There was only the soft murmur of the sea, over to his left. Finally, he stopped, trying to outwait his pursuers. Surely, if they were near, they would make some sound? Didn't the absolute lack of sound mean that they were far away?

One minute passed and then another. There was still no sound but Gilmore's nerves were now stretched taut. He was motionless, mainly because he could not summon the nerve to move. If he stayed completely still, he told himself, they would give up and go away. All he had to do was to remain utterly motionless.

To Gilmore, the snapping twig sounded like a pistol shot. Without any conscious volition, he shot to his feet and ran, panic-stricken, towards the beach.

Paul and Anton had been only yards away from Gilmore, Paul to landward, Anton to seaward. They had heard Gilmore's stealthy retreat and had gradually closed in on him, stopping whenever he stopped. When there had been no movement for almost three minutes, Paul had realised that their quarry was lying low. The solution was simple—he picked up a twig and snapped it cleanly in two.

Anton heard the snap of the twig and a second later saw Gilmore come hurtling out from behind a dune, heading to Anton's left. He moved across to intercept him.

At the last moment, Gilmore saw him and reacted surprisingly quickly. In one swift motion, he bent down, picked up a handful of sand and threw it in Anton's eyes with uncanny accuracy. Anton reeled back, blinded, as Gilmore pelted past him up the slope of the dune.

Paul saw Gilmore as he reached the crest of the dune, about thirty yards away. Paul muttered a curse. If he disappeared behind the dune, he might easily vanish for good. Panicked he might have been, but he had dealt very efficiently with Anton and would probably not fall for the same trick again. He had to be stopped.

All these thoughts flashed through Paul's mind in the time it took to raise his silenced Walther P38 pistol. He took aim, holding his right wrist with his left hand to steady it, and squeezed the trigger. There was a soft phut!

The bullet took Gilmore in the right shoulder, spinning him round so that he faced Paul, although he did not see him. Paul's second shot slammed into his chest, the impact hurling him backwards; his body rolled down the far slope in a tangle of arms and legs.

Gilmore was dead before he reached the bottom.

Paul looked down at the lifeless body and then at Anton. "Can you see properly now?"

"Yes." said Anton, wiping his eyes. "He certainly took me by surprise."

"He shouldn't have." Paul snapped. "If you had caught him, we could have disposed of him without leaving tell-tale bullet wounds. Before, if the local police had found him knifed or with a broken neck, they might well have thought of it as a local murder. But with two bullet wounds? They'd have to be damned stupid not to realise what's happened." He turned his head towards the sea, almost wistfully. "It's not the most auspicious start to a mission, is it?"

LONDON.

"Ah, Tyler. Good of you to come. Punctual as ever, I see. Do sit down."

Tyler did so, feeling a momentary twinge of envy as he looked around the oak-panelled office. Fenton had only recently been promoted but he had already succeeded in removing every trace of Charters, the previous occupant. Tyler did not begrudge the other man his advancement; Fenton was a first-class director of counter-intelligence operations, despite his nondescript appearance, which had been carefully cultivated during his ten years in the field with SIS. He had been transferred to MI5 four years before and had used his experience to good effect.

Fenton took his seat behind the large desk and regarded Tyler for several seconds. "This Markyate business. How is it progressing?"

"Not very well, I'm afraid, sir. We found two parachutes buried a quarter of a mile from where Lewis was found. We're still combing the area to see if there are any more, but nothing else has turned up so far. We've had half a dozen reports of so-called strangers boarding trains within walking distance of the killing, but the descriptions are next to useless. There's no guarantee that our two are among them in any case. Come to that, there could be more than two of them. They could be travelling separately or they might have had a rendezvous with someone who had transport available. They could be anywhere by now." He spread his hands, helplessly. "And that's about it, sir. That's all we have."

"Not even any speculations, Tyler?"

"Only one. The method used to kill Lewis—the garrotte. I think the murderer had specialist training."

"Like your own, Tyler?"

"Could well be, sir. It was one of the methods they taught us in the commandos. This killer knew what he was doing."

Fenton nodded. "Well, you should know if anyone does, Tyler." He swivelled his chair so that he could look out of the window. "I'd like a full written report ready for me by tomorrow morning. Include any speculations or theories you might have." He turned back to face Tyler and smiled briefly.

35

"Not my doing, actually. The Minister wishes to be kept fully appraised of the situation."

"The Minister?" asked Tyler, unable to keep the surprise out of his voice.

"Indeed. Our masters are somewhat concerned about this affair. I tell you this in order to emphasise its importance. We are all relying on you, Tyler, to find these spies."

All very well, thought Tyler, but there was no doubt who would be held responsible if things went wrong . . .

The Minister finished reading the final page of Tyler's report and placed it carefully on top of the other typed sheets on his desk. He opened a drawer and took out a briar pipe and a tobacco pouch. Fenton waited impassively as the pipe was tamped and lit; eventually, the Minister tapped the report.

"What's your opinion on this, Fenton? Is Tyler doing a good job so far?"

"He's being very thorough, sir. I cannot think of any line of enquiry that he is not pursuing."

"Not getting very far though, is he?"

"With respect, sir, he has very little to go on. These agents are professionals—they've left no clues behind at all."

"Yes. Tyler states that he believes the killer might have had commando style training. Do you agree with him or do you think he is jumping to conclusions?"

"He only mentions it as a possibility, sir," said Fenton defensively.

The Minister started levelly at Fenton and then re-lit his pipe. "What concerns me, Fenton, is Tyler's inexperience. He's only been with you for—what? Eighteen months? I know he had an excellent record in the Marines—rapid promotion to Captain, outstanding fitness reports, wounded in the St. Nazaire raid and then invalided out with a DSO. But it's not his courage I'm questioning, Fenton, it's his experience in counter-intelligence work. Should he be entrusted with an investigation like this?"

"He is an excellent officer, sir. He received training for

36

undercover work while he was in the Marines. He spent three months operating behind enemy lines in Crete and then two weeks in France reconnoitring St. Nazaire harbour for the raid. He knows all the tricks of the trade and his knowledge has stood him in very good stead. He's intelligent, resourceful and a very thorough investigator. In fact, I'd say he was one of the best men we've got."

"I hope you're right, Fenton. The PM is taking a personal interest in all this. He doesn't like the idea of Nazi agents running around the country killing civilians. He wants them caught and hanged. So, for your sake, Fenton, I hope you have chosen the right man. I really do."

LONDON.

Vogel looked at his watch. Nearly one o'clock. Just right, he hoped. He gave the operator the number he had been given as part of the operational briefing. A young woman's voice answered him.

"Can I speak to Sir David Menzies, please?"

"I'm very sorry. He's out to lunch. Who's calling, please?"

Vogel ignored the question. "Oh dear, that is a pity." Perfect, he thought. "Can you tell me when he'll be back?"

"Well, it's difficult to say. Who did you say you—"

"I see. Well, it is rather urgent," Vogel interrupted. "Is there anybody else I could speak to?"

"Well, there's Mr. Ferris. He might be able to help you, Mr.—?"

"Is that John Ferris?"

"Er, no. Michael."

"Oh yes, of course. I've already tried him. Is there anybody else?"

"Well, there's Mr. Lockhart, or Mr. Phillips. Mr. Rogers, but he's out to lunch as well. I'm sorry, sir, but I'm afraid I have to know your name before I put you through to anybody."

"But of course. My name—" Vogel pressed his finger down on the cradle, cutting her off. With any luck, she would think it was a fault on the line, common enough nowadays, as he had already discovered.

He smiled in satisfaction. He now had five names; he could start moving in. All that needed to be done was to put a face to one of the names, and the first step towards this was to consult the telephone directory. There was no listing for Menzies, the head of the department; presumably he was ex-directory. He ruled out Phillips and Rogers—there were too many listed in the directory. He considered both Lockhart and Ferris before deciding on the latter; there were only three entries under M. Ferris.

He was reasonably certain that Ferris would be on the phone, considering the nature of his work at Whitehall. All that needed to be done was to wait outside each of the three addresses in turn and follow each Ferris into work. With any luck, one of them would report to the office off Whitehall and they would have located one of the men who were responsible for organising Faust's schedules and itineraries.

There would still be a long way to go, but it was a start. Vogel was nothing if not patient.

Vogel stepped down from the bus as it was still slowing to a halt; Ferris, he knew, would be alighting behind him. He glanced around, making sure that there were no policemen about and also carrying out one last check of the area, although he knew the whole lay-out quite clearly. About thirty metres away was an alleyway, twenty metres long, enclosed by high walls. Ferris had used this alley as a short cut on his way home on both the previous occasions that Vogel had followed him. This was where the next stage of Vogel's plan would be carried out.

Vogel turned into the alley and went halfway along it before halting. He reached into his jacket pocket, took out a packet of cigarettes and turned to face the wall. He lit a cigarette, cupping his hands around the match's flame as he did so; the movement also concealed his features.

Ferris only half-noticed him. He was almost home. Eve had said it would be liver tonight—she had managed to charm some out of the local butcher. Liver was a particular favourite of Ferris'.

He passed Vogel without looking at him at all, still preoccupied with thoughts of dinner. He heard a movement behind him and then he felt a paralysing pain in the back of his neck. He was vaguely aware of the ground coming up to meet him, but he never remembered actually hitting it . . .

Expertly, Vogel searched Ferris. He found a wallet and removed several banknotes from it. Vogel gave a sigh of relief as he found Ferris' diary. He flicked through the pages until he found the Addresses section then he quickly scanned the neat, precise writing.

"Phillips," he read, memorising the address. Further down, he found Lockhart's address and committed that to memory as well. There was no sign of an entry for Rogers. He replaced the diary and stood up. He walked away, not seeming to hurry, but within seconds he was out in the street.

The entire incident had taken less than thirty seconds. Ferris would wake up in five or ten minutes, find the money missing from his wallet, and would come to the obvious conclusion; a straightforward robbery, nothing more. He would probably report it to the Police, but Vogel was certain that he hadn't seen his face.

Another step closer to Faust.

CHAPTER 3

The girl was the subject of a good deal of male attention in the bar as she accompanied McConville over to the corner table where Vogel sat waiting. It was not surprising, thought Vogel; she was certainly a very attractive girl. McConville had done well . . .

"Hallo, Ken. How are you?"

"Couldn't be better. You?"

"Just fine. May I introduce Miss Maureen Riordan? Maureen, this is Kenneth Vernon, an old friend of mine."

"Delighted to meet you," said Vogel, standing up.

She smiled. "Thank you, Mr. Vernon."

"What'll it be?" asked McConville.

"A gin and bitters," the girl replied. Vogel asked for a pint. While the Irishman was at the bar, Vogel and the girl sat appraising each other.

Maureen Riordan was even more startlingly attractive close to. She was about twenty-five, tall, with long dark hair and green eyes. As she removed her nondescript coat, he could see that she had a superb figure as well.

"Well?" she said, calmly. "Do I pass?"

"Oh yes," he replied, not in the least discomfited. "Has Sean told you anything?"

"Only that you were an old friend of his, and that I was under your orders."

"How do you feel about that?"

"I have no opinions about it, Mr. Vernon. I just obey my orders."

40

"Even from me?"

"Even from you."

"We'll get along splendidly," he said, with a faint smile, just as McConville returned with the drinks.

"Well?" he asked.

"Just what the doctor ordered," Vogel answered.

"Good," said McConville.

"What exactly do you want with me?" Maureen asked.

Vogel looked her squarely in the eyes. "I want you to seduce a man you haven't even met yet."

Her eyes flashed momentarily, flickered once to McConville and then came back to Vogel. They were steady again. "Right," she said, calmly. "When?"

"Within the next week or so."

"I see."

"Do you live by yourself?"

"Yes. I have a flat in Kilburn."

"And what do you do for a living?"

"I work as a secretary to—a friend of Sean's." Vogel did not miss the momentary hesitation.

He turned to McConville. "Can your 'friend' spare her?"

"He will, if I say so."

"Good." He turned back to Maureen. "You will have to be available at all times, you see."

"Right," she said.

Vogel looked at her consideringly, before asking his next question in a flat monotone. "How many men have you slept with?"

Her eyes flared. "What the hell has that got to do with you?"

"Everything, believe me. I don't just want you to seduce him, I want him to enjoy it so much, he won't be thinking straight. I need to know how good you are in bed."

"You don't mince words, do you?"

Vogel shrugged.

41

"Six, altogether," she said quietly.

"That's better," he said. "Were any of them because of orders you were given?"

"Yes," she said, even more quietly.

"I need to be absolutely certain you can do it, that's all."

Her voice gained force. "Sean told me you were a very important man, that you were engaged on very important business. I won't let you down, Mr. Vernon. If it helps The Cause, it'll be an honour, I assure you."

Vogel was impressed, despite himself. "Right, you're on the team." He turned to McConville. "Where can she be briefed?"

McConville thought. "Her flat?"

"All right by you?" Vogel asked Maureen.

"Fine."

McConville looked at Vogel. "Will you want me there?"

Vogel had already debated whether to include McConville in the operation and had reluctantly decided against it. Ultimately, McConville's first loyalty would be to the IRA, not to Vogel, despite the 'debt' he owed. "Afraid not, Sean."

"I thought as much," said McConville, philosophically.

Her flat was neat and compact. She offered Vogel a cup of tea, which he accepted, relaxing in an old but comfortable armchair.

"Right, what exactly do I have to do?" she asked.

"We are observing four or five men at the monent. I want you to seduce one of them."

"Any particular one?"

"That's up to you."

"Really? I have a choice?"

"In a way, yes. I want you to choose the one that will be the most amenable."

"By amenable, do you mean the one most likely to give in to blackmail?"

"Exactly."

"You'll be taking photographs?"

Vogel nodded. He noticed the distaste on her face. "You have an objection?"

"Of course I bloody do, but that doesn't mean I'm not prepared to do it."

"Are you absolutely certain of that?"

"I told you in the pub that I'd do it, didn't I? I've done it before, after all."

"You were working directly for the IRA then. This time you're not."

"McConville gave me an order. That's good enough for me," she snapped. She saw his sceptical expression and continued heatedly, "Look, my father and mother were killed by the Black and Tans in Belfast. I was brought up by my grandparents, who were staunch IRA supporters, so I've lived and breathed the cause of a United Ireland for as long as I can remember. I hate those British bastards and I'd do anything—anything, you understand?—to hit back at them. So, Mr. Vernon, or whatever your name is, if my superior officer orders me to seduce a man then, by God, I'll do it!" Her eyes were blazing at him. "And don't you dare question my devotion to The Cause again!"

Vogel stared intently at her and nodded. "I accept the rebuke," he said calmly. "You've convinced me."

Her eyes, still furious, held his for several seconds and then she looked away. She took a deep breath; when she spoke, her voice was brisk, businesslike. "Will it be just for one night, or over a period of time?"

"Well, put it this way. The more evidence we can confront him with, the more likely he will be to do what we ask him."

"So it'll be more than once."

"I'm afraid so."

Surprisingly, she smiled. "Don't apologise. For all you know, I might enjoy every minute of it."

"Quite possibly," agreed Vogel, equably; she saw the folly of trying to throw him off balance. He continued, "What is more important is that he enjoys it so much that he will be desperate for more."

"Right," she shrugged. "You're in command."

Vogel gave her a long, lingering look, that took in her slim figure. "Am I?" he said, with a faint smile.

Randall came into Tyler's office, looking excited. "This just came in. It was referred to us by the duty officer. It's from Suffolk County Police."

"Suffolk? We're interested in Hertfordshire, not Suffolk."

"Wait till you hear this. They've found a body of a man who had been shot twice. He was killed at about 2.30 in the morning on a particularly deserted stretch of coast north of Aldeburgh. Night before last."

Tyler looked up, showing interest for the first time. "I suppose it took them that long to get through official channels, did it?"

"It would have taken longer, but the bullets were identified as German. Probably a Walther automatic."

"Good God."

"The ballistic report states that he was shot from a range of about thirty yards, by somebody about twenty feet below him. He was apparently found at the foot of a sand-dune."

"So he was probably at the top when he was shot. Whoever shot him must have been shooting uphill, at a range of thirty yards, at night. Damn good shooting," he concluded, with an air of professional approval.

"That's what the ballistics experts reckon as well, sir. Apparently, the first shot hit the victim on the right shoulder from behind, which presumably spun him round. The second was right in the heart."

"He'd need to be an ace marksman to do all that. That clinches it. The victim—"

"Gilmore. John Gilmore."

"—must have seen something, went to investigate and got shot for his pains. Trouble is, the killer'll be miles away by now. It can't be coincidence. It must tie in with this Hertfordshire thing." He paused, stared at the map on the wall and frowned. "Thing is, if it's connected with

44

Hertfordshire, why send him in separately? It doubles the risk of detection, having two groups, after all."

"Perhaps it's a separate operation altogether."

"Unlikely. They wouldn't send in two of them within a few days. There'd be too much chance of one queering the other group's pitch. So, if they're connected, why send in a marksman a week later?"

"They don't have to be connected," persisted Randall. "Could be a case of two separate departments not knowing what the other one's doing. Let's face it, we're always treading on Special Branch's corns."

"Correction. It's Special Branch who tread on our corns, but I take your point. One could be Abwehr, the other from RSHA Amt IV. Whichever it is, one group or two, there's still a trained Jerry marksman on the loose." He paused, as a further thought struck him. He stared out of the window.

Randall broke the silence. "If he is an assassin—"

"Exactly. Who is he after?"

Paul had finally found lodgings in Hampstead, a part of London he knew fairly well; his parents had lived in Hendon for five years.

He had taken a room with the Marriott family. Mr. Marriott had served in the first War, being wounded at Ypres; his campaign medals were kept proudly displayed on the mantelpiece. Marriott now worked as a clerk at the Handley Page factory at Cricklewood but was doggedly reticent about his work, maintaining darkly that "Walls have ears". Paul wondered, in idle moments, how Mr. Marriott would have reacted had he known that his lodger was an Abwehr agent.

Mrs. Marrtiott was a tiny wisp of a woman, who, Paul guessed, had been very attractive once but who now looked permanently tired, as if the effort of producing substantial meals for her undeniably overweight husband over the years had worn her out.

There was a daughter as well, Carolyn. Paul had already decided to avoid her if at all possible. Carolyn Marriott was in her early twenties, and very sexually aware; she had already given him several meaningful looks, full of frank invitation. Paul had to admit she was very attractive, with long, blonde hair (dyed? he wondered) and deep blue eyes. At any other time, Paul would have welcomed her interest, even encouraged it. But not now.

He lay back on the bed and stared at the ceiling. How was he going to find Vogel? It was safest to assume that Vogel, somehow, would find out all about Faust's movements. To do that he would have to approach people in Whitehall, directly or indirectly; Paul would have to know when that happened, and the only way he could find that out would be through 'Jaguar', the Abwehr agent in London. There was even a remote chance that Vogel had been instructed to approach 'Jaguar' in any case, but Paul doubted if he would. Like himself, Vogel would be reluctant to use an agent whose only loyalty was to the money he was being paid; such men had been known to change sides too easily. No, Vogel would avoid 'Jaguar'. but Paul had no choice in the matter; he had to use the agent if he was to have any chance at all of tracking Vogel down.

There was a knock at the door. As he expected, it was Carolyn.

"Fancy a cup of tea? I've just made one."

"I'd love one, thank you."

"Oh, good. I'll go and bring one up."

"Oh, there's no need. I was just coming down, anyway."

Maureen put down the set of photographs and looked at Vogel. "So this is the one?"

Vogel nodded.

She picked up the last photo and regarded it thoughtfully. "He's not all that bad looking," she said. "Tell me about him."

"His name is Michael Lockhart. He is twenty-seven years old and he is a Civil Servant working in Whitehall. What exactly he does need not concern you at the moment. He is a bachelor, but he is engaged to a young woman called Claire Hamilton." Vogel opened the briefcase he had brought with him and passed over another photograph. "That's her."

She studied it. "She doesn't look anything special. Rather plain, really. I'd've thought he could have done better than that."

"Her father is a very senior Civil Servant in the Home Office."

"I see. He's marrying into influence."

"Exactly. Lockhart is very ambitious but he comes from an undistinguished background—apparently he rarely talks about it. He gained very good results at University, however, but it wasn't Oxford or Cambridge. He didn't go to the right school either, so to get ahead, he has to have contacts in high places. Which is where Miss Hamilton comes in. They've been engaged for two years and it seems to have worked for him—he's being promoted on September 1st. The wedding is two months after that."

"You know a lot about him."

He smiled faintly. "It's my job to find out things about people."

She tapped the photograph. "I can see that any scandal would ruin his marriage and his career. So what makes you think he'd be susceptible to seduction?"

"Frankly, Miss Riordan, I find it hard to believe that he will resist your advances. You are a remarkably attractive young woman." He was not paying her a compliment, she realised, merely stating a fact. He continued, "In addition, there is no evidence that his relationship with his fiancée is a sexual one. They appear to be observing all the proprieties: he would not dare do otherwise, I imagine. But if the opportunity for a discreet affaire were to present itself and if the woman involved were sufficiently desirable . . ."

"I see what you mean. A way of easing the frustration?"

"Exactly."

She studied his photograph again. "Well, I could have done worse," she acknowledged. "So when does it all take place?"

"As soon as possible."

"I'll see what I can do. Do you want me to bring him here, or do you have somewhere else in mind?"

47

"Here if possible. May I see your bedroom?"

She led the way into the bedroom and Vogel looked rapidly around the room, sizing it up. The bed faced the door, with a dressing table against the left hand wall, opposite the window. There was a large wardrobe next to the window. On the other side of the window was a bedside table and a small wooden chair in front of the dressing table.

Vogel opened the capacious wardrobe. It had a large ornamental brass handle on each door. He pointed to them. "Can these be removed?"

"I should think so."

"Good. We should be able to put in a spyhole big enough for the lens."

"Won't it be noticeable?"

Vogel smiled, sardonically. "Miss Riordan, if you do your job properly, I doubt very much that he will be examining ornamental handles very closely."

"True," admitted Maureen. With a camera situated there, the photographs would show a side-on view of the bed, from only a yard or so away. She and her partner would be about four or five feet from the camera. "What exactly do you want to film?"

"You and the man, in as many compromising positions as possible. It's vital that his face be clearly shown; it doesn't matter whether yours is or not. Try to make him face the camera, if you can."

"I'll do my best."

"I'm sure you will."

Paul saw 'Jaguar' standing beside the Serpentine, a small, neatly dressed man in the Civil Service uniform of pinstripe suit and bowler hat. He seemed to represent the epitome of British respectability, to be a pillar of society; as Paul well knew, he had been working for the Abwehr for two years.

"Sorry I'm late," said Paul, using the code introduction.

'Jaguar' looked up. "Actually, I'm early." He tossed some bread to the ducks. "How can I help you?"

"Supposing I wished to find out the future itineraries of a leading member of the Government, how would I go about it?"

If 'Jaguar' was surprised by the question, he showed no signs of it. He thought for a few moments before answering. "There's a small department, run by Sir David Menzies, which handles itineraries for all non-military VIPs. they liaise with the Press."

"Would it be difficult to find details of any given person's schedule?"

"It would be, if you're an ordinary member of the public. They only release details to accredited members of the Press and even then, it's generally only twenty four hours beforehand. In any case, it's only for planned journeys and visits. Quite often, of course, impromptu visits are arranged, especially to bomb damaged areas. Good for public morale, you see." The bitterness in his voice was only too evident. "Which VIP did you have in mind?"

"I wish I knew," Paul confessed. "Somebody will be after information concerning a specific VIP. Is there any way you could find out if any member of this department is being tapped for information?"

'Jaguar' gave Paul a searching look, as if trying to figure out why he should want to know that. Was there a high ranking agent, about whom he knew nothing, that they were trying to protect? Pointless to speculate; something told him that this stranger would only tell him if he needed to know. "Possibly," he replied, at length. "I know Menzies quite well. I'll look into it."

"This department, it's for civilians only?"

"Yes. Military VIPs are handled by a military liaison group at the Admiralty. I don't see how I could make enquiries into that at the moment."

"Fair enough. I don't think it'll be necessary, anyway."

"If I have any news for you, do I contact you through 'Lynx'?"

'Lynx' was the codename of the Abwehr radio operator in London; Paul nodded.

"Will he be able to contact you quickly if the message is urgent?"

"I'll get the message in plenty of time, never fear."

'Jaguar' smiled faintly. "In other words, you're making sure that I have no idea where you are or how to contact you."

"It's safer that way," said Paul.

"Oh, don't misunderstand me. I fully approve. I like working with professionals. It makes me feel safer."

"So do I," replied Paul. The trouble is, he thought, 'Jaguar' is only an amateur.

Maureen recognised Lockhart as soon as he emerged from the Whitehall building at a few minutes after five. He was very smartly dressed in an expensive looking pinstripe suit; every inch the rising Civil Servant. She watched him as he looked up and down, searching for a taxi. He invariably used a taxicab to travel to and from the office; he would not want to be seen catching a bus. She went up to him.

"Excuse me?" she said.

"Er—yes?"

"Are you waiting for a taxi?"

"Yes I am, actually."

"You wouldn't be going anywhere near Kilburn, would you?"

She could see the sudden interest in his eyes. "Indeed I am. Would you like to share mine?"

She smiled attractively. "Well, they're always telling us to do that if we can, aren't they? I'd love to, Mr.—?"

"Lockhart. Michael Lockhart." He held out his hand.

She took it. "Maureen Riordan."

He stepped forward suddenly as he saw a taxi; he felt obscurely pleased as it drew to a halt. He held the door for her and then climbed in after her. "We'll drop you off first, shall we. Where to?"

She gave her address and the taxi drove off. She glanced at the driver and then leaned over towards Lockhart. "Maybe you'll be able to tell me if he's going the long way round? I don't really know my way about London yet."

"Certainly," he smiled. "Have you not been in London very long?"

"No. Less than a month. As you've probably guessed, I'm from Northern Ireland."

"What do you think of London, then?"

"Big. I keep getting lost. I don't really know anyone, you see." She smiled and drew in her breath so that her breasts were thrust outwards. She was wearing a blouse and skirt that showed off her figure to good advantage and she saw his eyes suddenly narrow; he seemed to be mentally undressing her. "It'd be nice if I knew someone who could show me around," she said softly, her voice laden with invitation.

She saw his momentary hesitation and felt a stab of doubt: had 'Vernon' been wrong after all? Then he smiled and she relaxed; it was going to be all right.

"May I offer my services as a guide? Perhaps we could go for a drink, maybe a meal, and I could show you the sights?"

"Why, that would be lovely—Michael." Hook, line and sinker, she thought.

CHAPTER 4

Michael Lockhart stared at his reflection in the mirror as he finished shaving. He was thinking about the forthcoming evening, wondering whether he was being a damned fool taking Maureen out for a drink. There would be the devil to pay if Claire or her father ever heard about it. It would almost certainly result in the marriage being called off and in his promotion being rescinded. He was well aware that the one depended on the other; he was risking his entire future for a possible night of passion with a girl who meant nothing to him.

On the other hand, thought Lockhart, Maureen Riordan was a remarkably desirable woman. If she delivered only half what her eyes had promised, it would still be sensational . . . especially after two years of living like a monk. Until his engagement to Claire, Lockhart had led an active sex life but all that had ended the moment he had realised that Claire Hamilton held the key to his future. Their relationship had not progressed beyond occasional stealthy kisses; Claire would not dream of allowing it to go any further and Lockhart was far too interested in what her father could do for him to risk offending her.

And it had worked; his promotion had come through and he knew that it had been Sir Charles Hamilton's doing. At last, after repeated requests for a transfer, he was finally escaping the department and its time servers. It was not before time; there had been absolutely no prospect of any advancement from such a dead-end appointment otherwise.

Although Lockhart was being rather over-critical of the department and its members, there was a good deal of truth in what he felt. Although their work was important, in that they co-ordinated and planned itineraries for VIPs who might conceivably be targets for assassins, it was true that, as the war had progressed, Menzies' group had decreased in priority. There had not been even the merest suspicion of an assassination attempt on any leading British figure since the beginning of the war and so, gradually, the work of the department became increasingly routine. The high security classification personnel who had originally formed the group had been transferred to areas which seemed to need their talents more. By 1944, Menzies apart—and he was purely a figurehead—the entire staff of the department consisted of worthy Civil Servants with blameless records but with little to recommend them, save efficiency. It had not been a conscious policy; it had simply been that there had been no need for tight security to be imposed on the department. Security had relaxed by default, more than by any conscious policy. Lockhart, like his colleagues, had an adequate security classification but he was not a security expert; the need for that had never arisen. As far as Lockhart was concerned, the job was simply that of a filing clerk; but now it would soon be over for him. Providing he kept his nose clean . . .

He began to dress, still debating whether he should run the risk of meeting Maureen. It should be safe enough, he told himself; she lived in Kilburn, a comfortable social distance away from Knightsbridge and Claire, and so the odds of him being seen by any mutual acquaintances were remote, provided he avoided certain places . . . And she was a stunningly beautiful girl. Lockhart had a vivid mental image of Maureen lying naked on a bed, holding out her arms to him. It had been two years since he had last been with a woman like that; didn't he owe himself one last fling before he tied himself to Claire for good? He looked at her photograph on the dressing table; poor Claire, he thought, but without sympathy. She looked even less attractive than usual when compared to Maureen.

That settled it; the thought of missing out on the promised pleasures of Maureen's body became even more intolerable when measured against the prospect of the wedding night with Claire. Lockhart fastened his tie and looked at his watch; he should be in plenty of time to meet Maureen at eight o'clock.

Maureen switched on the light and closed the door. "Well, here it is," she said. "Not much, but it's home."

Lockhart barely noticed the flat or its furnishings; he had eyes only for her, wondering if the veiled invitations and half-promises were to be fulfilled. There was a tight knot of tension in his stomach; he was breathless with a combination of doubt and excited anticipation. Two years of celibacy had taken their toll; he could not remember being so nervous before.

"Do sit down, Michael," she said, gesturing at the sofa. "I'll get you that drink I promised you. Whisky, wasn't it?"

"Please," he said hoarsely as he sat down.

She poured two glasses and then sat next to him on the sofa. They touched glasses. "Cheers," she said. "And thank you for a lovely evening, Michael."

"The pleasure was all mine, Maureen. Perhaps we could do it again?"

"I'd love to."

"Soon?" Warning bells were ringing at the back of his mind; don't take chances, there was too much risk involved. At the moment, however, Claire Hamilton seemed to be part of another existence.

"Soon," she echoed, nodding. Their eyes met and he could see the invitation written plainly there. Lockhart set down his glass on the coffee table and she leaned across him to do the same, her perfume exciting him still further. The instant she released the glass, he pulled her to him, his lips searching hungrily for hers. Her response was immediate; her arms drew him closer and she gave a soft moan.

Quickly, eagerly, he unfastened her blouse, reaching inside to cup her brassiered breast as he pushed her down onto the sofa. Their lips were still pressed tightly together; his hand moved onto her thigh, pushing up under her skirt in frantic haste. His fingers touched the bare skin above her stockings, the almost forgotten sensation causing him to gasp involuntarily. He wanted her, he had to have her . . .

Her mouth twisted free of his. "Hey . . . hey! Gently, lover . . . gently." There was a challenging smile on her lips; she was obviously not displeased by the way he had responded.

"Not so fast." She wriggled out from underneath him and stood up as he stared at her, confused: was she just a tease, after all?

"Just give me a couple of minutes to get ready, lover." She unbuttoned her blouse and slowly, provocatively, slipped it off her slim shoulders. "Two minutes," she said huskily and then turned away from him. His eyes followed her as she went into the bedroom.

Lockhart let out his breath in a long sigh. He stood up and went over to the sideboard to pour himself a large measure of whisky. It went down in one gulp. Two years had definitely been too long, he decided; but he would make up for it tonight . . .

"Michael," she called. "I'm ready." He heard her give a low chuckle. "Come and get it."

The sight that greeted him in the bedroom made him draw in his breath sharply. The light was still on and she was lying on the bed, absolutely naked. He stood there for several seconds, spellbound, taking in every detail of her and then she arched her body slowly, languidly, in invitation. "Come on, Michael," she moaned, holding out her arms to him. "I want you."

Just as he had imagined it would be . . . Lockhart pushed the door closed behind him and moved towards the bed.

Maureen opened the wardrobe door. "He's gone," she said, quietly. She had put on a dark blue dressing gown.

Vogel emerged slowly, wincing from the ache in his back, caused by the cramped way he had been crouching for the last couple of hours.

"Did you get the photos?" she asked.

"I should dam' well hope so," Vogel replied. He looked at her, noticing her flushed cheeks and aware of a stirring in his groin—hardly surprising, when one considered what he had been watching. Lockhart had been like a man who had just emerged from a desert and then found himself confronted by a pool of fresh spring water; his enthusiasm and stamina had been impressive, to say the least.

"I could do with a drink," she said, her voice hoarse. "How about you?" His expression sent a shiver down her spine. There was an animal magnetism about him that she found incredibly arousing, even at a moment like this. Or perhaps, she realised, it was because of the last two hours; Vogel had witnessed everything she had done with Lockhart. Her awareness of his presence had both inhibited and excited her. She wanted Vogel to take his already intimate knowledge of her body to its final conclusion.

Vogel looked into her eyes and saw the unmistakeable invitation there. The memory of how her naked body had looked on the bed came into his mind; why not? he thought.

Not yet, he told himself. Only when the time is right. "Maybe another time," he said, brusquely.

Maureen shot him a venomous look as he turned away. Don't you be so sure there will be another time, she thought, furious and frustrated at the rejection. I only ever offer once, damn you! You won't get any more chances!

Deep down, she knew she lied . . .

"Come in, Tyler. Please sit down."

Tyler did so, noting the new painting hanging behind Fenton's desk; it looked like a Constable but he had no way of knowing if it was genuine. Fenton was certainly making himself at home . . .

"Any further progress with your mystery German paratroopers, Tyler?"

"None at all, I'm afraid, sir. We've had a few more people who've come forward with descriptions of suspects but nothing to indicate where they went. We're trying to match these descriptions up with railway staff at main line stations, but it's a pretty hopeless task."

Fenton nodded. "I see. And what about this business at Aldeburgh?"

"Again, nothing. No witnesses, no further clues found at the scene."

"But you think the two incidents are connected?"

Tyler shrugged. "They could be. In one group, the Markyate one, there's someone who's a dab hand with a garrotte. And Gilmore was killed by a trained marksman, so that would seem to be a connection, but why send them separately? That's the bit I can't figure out."

"They might be sending in two separate groups to double their chances of success."

"It also doubles the chances of being detected."

"True. And you think they could be on an assassination mission?"

"Could well be. We have at least two killers involved, both of whom appear to be highly trained."

Fenton stared thoughtfully out of the window. "I'm afraid you could well be right, Tyler . . . We'd better put this search on a large scale. I'll put you in overall command with direct access to Scotland Yard and to any files you may consider necessary."

"Thank you," said Tyler, with no hint of expression in his voice. It was not a responsibility he relished.

Fenton continued, "I may be able to offer some help, however. There may well be a contact for these agents in London."

"We don't know of any."

"True. However, for some months now, there has been a suspicion that we do have an enemy agent in our midst. No more than a suspicion, however, and, if truth be told, it was nothing much more than a vague disquiet. We now have reason to believe that there is an agent working for the Germans and that he is quite high up in the Home Office.

"To try and identify this agent we have deliberately been channelling false information through various departments to see if any of it reached the Germans; we have several contacts within the Abwehr and even a couple in the SS."

Get on with it, for God's sake, thought Tyler. Stop beating about the bush.

"We've finally turned up trumps, so to speak, and the nature of the information passed has enabled us to draw up a list of four suspects." Fenton pushed a large manila folder across the desk to Tyler. "These four, in fact."

Tyler stared at the bulky folder. "What exactly do you intend, sir?"

"Investigate them, Tyler. Keep a watch on them. We would have to do this in any case but it may well help you; if you can identify our traitor, then you might have a lead to your killers."

Tyler felt that this was unlikely, that it was a very long shot indeed, but he also had to admit that he had nothing else to go on. "How many men can I have, sir?"

"Use your entire Section. This is very urgent, Tyler. These men have access to virtually unlimited information."

"So I gather," said Tyler, leafing through the file. "Do I have a free hand?"

"Naturally."

"Then I'd better get on with it, hadn't I?"

Paul paused at the door, a sixth sense warning him. He knew, intuitively, that someone was inside his room. He took a deep breath and pushed the door open.

Carolyn was standing by the dressing table, a duster in her hand. "Oh, hallo, Mr. Keen. I hope you don't mind. I just thought I'd give your room a dust."

"Thank you," he replied, smiling to show he didn't mind. "But there's no need."

"Oh, it's alright," she said, smiling in turn. "I didn't have much else to do."

Had she been looking through his belongings? It wouldn't matter much if she had, Paul reminded himself. There was nothing incriminating amongst his baggage but it was difficult to ignore the almost instinctive fear of the unexpected. Possibly, she had indeed been looking but not through suspicion; her interest in him was purely sexual.

"Well, it's awfully kind of you," he said.

"Any time," she said, lightly. "Like I said, there's not much to do when I'm at home at the weekend."

Her every word seemed loaded with invitation. Paul ignored the momentary vision of how he could take ådvantage of the situation and merely commented, "Really?"

"No. I mean, there's not much you can do in the evening. Anyone would think there was a war on or something."

Paul grinned. "True." She was leaning against the dressing table, her shoulders pulled back so that he could hardly fail to notice her breasts. He forced himself to look away. "Still, it'll soon be over, I expect."

"You think so?"

"Yes, I do. Now we've invaded France, I don't think the Jerries can last much longer." As he spoke, he found himself wondering: who was 'we' as far as he was concerned? Whose side was he on?

"It'll be funny," she was saying. "Peace, I mean. I was eighteen when the war began. But now—well, some of my friends from school are married with kids. Mum keeps on to me about getting married, but I don't think it's right. Not with a war on. I mean, I could marry someone and he could be dead the next day. Then there's the kids. Family round in Mitchell Drive, their house was hit by a bomb. They all died, both parents, and a two year old kid. I mean, what sort of life did that kid have? No, it isn't right, having kids when there's a war on."

Paul found himself mentally revising his opinion of her; she was more intelligent than he'd first thought.

"So I'm not getting married," she said. "At least, not until the war's over, no matter what Mum says."

Dear God, thought Paul, the British are winning this war and she's saying things like that. If what she says is true, and I can't honestly disagree with her, then what about the German children who were still being born? What sort of life would they have after the war once the Allies had crushed Germany? What had that madman Hitler brought them to? And what was he, Paul, doing here on a mission that he claimed could have no effect on the war's outcome? Why wasn't he back in Germany, plotting to kill the madman, instead of risking his life on a wild goose chase?

And then he thought of Vogel.

And he knew why.

Maureen was putting on her make-up when she heard the knock on the door. She frowned; who could it be? She was not expecting 'Vernon', but it would be just like him to arrive unannounced. Putting on a dressing gown, she went to answer the door.

It was not Vernon at all, however; it was McConville. He smiled at her. "Evening, Maureen. Can I come in?"

"Oh—yes, of course."

McConville looked around as he came in. "Not disturbing you, am I?" he asked, looking at her dressing gown.

She flushed at the implication. "Well—not at the moment, but I do have to go out soon."

"I shan't keep you long, don't worry. I'd just like to ask you a few questions about Vernon and what he's up to."

"Certainly, sir." She sat down on the sofa.

"Have you managed to find out what he's up to?"

"Well, as you guessed, sir, it's a blackmail operation."

"Who's the victim?"

"A Michael Lockhart. He's a junior Civil Servant."

"And what does Vernon want him to do?"

She shook her head. "I don't know. He hasn't told me."

"No, I don't suppose he has," said McConville, almost to himself. "Have you—ah—met Lockhart yet?"

"If you mean have I seduced him yet, then yes. Vernon was in the wardrobe photographing the whole thing."

McConville could hear the distaste in her voice and nodded sympathetically. "What does Lockhart do in the Civil Service, then?"

"He works for the Home Office. He's basically just a filing clerk, although he tries to give the impression that he's more important than that. He's apparently engaged and is relying on his marriage to gain promotion."

"Which is what Vernon will be working on. But what does Lockhart actually do? What does he know that is so important?"

"I don't know, sir. He doesn't say much about his work—

he's too busy trying to get my knickers off most of the time," she said, disgustedly.

McConville ignored her comment. "Right, Maureen. This is what I want you to do. Try to get Lockhart to talk about what he does, what sort of documents he has access to, that sort of thing. But don't let Vernon know what you're up to, for God's sake. I want to know just what Vernon is planning, so anything you can find out, pass it on directly to me. You know where I can be contacted?"

She nodded. "What about Vernon himself? Do I try to get him to tell me what he's going to do?"

McConville smiled tautly. "You can try, Maureen, but it won't do you any good. You won't get anything out of him that he doesn't want you to know. No, you concentrate on Lockhart. The minute you find out anything, you let me know. Understood?"

"Yes, sir."

"Good. I'll leave you to get ready then."

As he descended the steps leading down to the street, McConville did not notice the tall man waiting at the bus stop on the far side of the road about thirty yards away. Even if McConville had noticed him, he would have been unlikely to recognise the other man; Vogel was wearing a hat with its brim pulled well down and was apparently lighting a cigarette, his cupped hands covering his face.

As McConville reached the foot of the steps and turned to walk in the opposite direction, Vogel dropped the cigarette and ground it out with his shoe. He looked thoughtfully at McConville's retreating back. This development had not been entirely unexpected; Vogel had kept Maureen's flat under periodic surveillance for precisely this reason, but it was still unwelcome. Perhaps it had been too much to hope for that McConville would not try to find out what was going on, but the last thing Vogel wanted was to have the IRA interfering with his operation in any way. He would have to deal with this changed situation, but he had already made plans for just this contingency.

61

It was a pity, really; Vogel had almost come to like McConville.

'Jaguar' turned around as Paul greeted him. He looked vaguely startled; he had not heard Paul's approach at all.

Paul had only just received the relayed message via 'Lynx' asking him to meet 'Jaguar'. Paul was surprised; he didn't think 'Jaguar' would turn anything up so quickly. "Well?" he asked. "Do you have some information?"

"Nothing definite." He raised his hand to forestall Paul's impatient retort. "Just something I witnessed that may be significant." He paused and absently tossed a few crumbs of bread into the middle of the circling ducks.

Paul was irritated. One of the problems of dealing with an agent like 'Jaguar' was that the source was often very garrulous with his contact. It was understandable. Such an agent might spend years metaphorically looking over his shoulder, having to watch everything he said, never really being able to relax, never able to confide in anyone. When he met someone aware of his true identity, there was often an irresistible urge to talk, to unburden himself. Paul had seen it before; it was generally a sign that the agent was near the end of his tether. If he felt the urge to talk, then he would eventually do so, but to the wrong person . . . Paul wasn't sure if this was the case here or if 'Jaguar' had genuine information. Either way, he had no alternative but to listen.

"I was over in Swiss Cottage the night before last. Visiting a lady friend, actually. I took her for a drink."

Paul groaned inwardly. It looked as though 'Jaguar' had nothing useful to tell him after all.

"The thing is, I saw someone I knew vaguely. Chap called Lockhart. He was coming out of the pub just as we were arriving and he was with a very attractive young lady. Unfortunately this young lady was not the one he is engaged to. He looked very embarrassed and hurried out with her."

Paul was exasperated. Was this all 'Jaguar' had? None of his thoughts showed in his expression, however. "I take it Lockhart would have access to the schedules we're interested in?"

"Oh yes, certainly. The point is that if his fiancée or future father-in-law were to find out, he'd be finished. His career depends on his marriage, you see. He's taking a dreadful risk if he is actually having an affaire with this girl."

Bloody fool, thought Paul. What was the idiot thinking of? That the girl would seduce Lockhart and make him reveal everything? Blackmail him? It was vaguely possible, Paul conceded, but where would Vogel get the girl? A prostitute? Too risky; there would be too much chance the girl would realise what was going on. Obviously, 'Jaguar' thought the girl might be some sort of Mata Hari, but it just wasn't on. He couldn't say so to 'Jaguar', of course. Highly placed sources like the man beside him had to be cosseted, told how important they were, even if ninety five per cent of their material was useless. It was the other five per cent you were paying for.

"It might well be," he agreed.

"Shall I look into it, discreetly?"

"By all means," said Paul absently.

"I'll see what I can find out about Lockhart and his Irish girlfriend, then. Maybe—"

"Did you say she was Irish?" asked Paul suddenly.

"Yes, I did."

"Are you certain she's Irish?"

"Absolutely. Lockhart had to introduce us—didn't like it, but he didn't have much choice. Her name is Maureen Riordan and she has a lovely Irish brogue."

And, at last, Paul was interested.

Anton was already in the pub when Paul arrived. They took their drinks to a corner table. "We'll have to be careful, if we're going to make a habit of meeting in pubs," observed Paul. "We could end up as alcoholics."

"Not on this stuff," commented Anton after a preliminary sip. He had received the message from Paul via the telephone contact that afternoon but had no idea why he had been summoned; however, he knew that Paul would have some specific object in mind and would broach it in his own time.

"We may have a lead on Vogel," said Paul, quietly.

Anton showed no reaction whatsoever; Paul had not expected him to—he was a professional, like himself.

"Really?"

"A possibility," amended Paul. "I want you to put a Michael Lockhart under surveillance. He works at an office in Whitehall. I'll give you the address later."

"You think he's a contact?"

"No. I'm more interested in his girlfriend. She's apparently very attractive, so I don't suppose you'll have any trouble identifying her. I want you to switch your attention to her, keep her under observation. I'll relieve you every so often."

"Why is she so important?"

"Apparently, Lockhart has access to schedules that Vogel would probably be very interested in. Whoever Faust is, he could find out his planned itineraries from them. Lockhart's new girlfriend is Irish and Vogel has contacts with the IRA, particularly with a Sean McConville, so there might be a link. Vogel might have contacted them."

"Rather a long shot, isn't it?"

"I know that," Paul conceded. "On the other hand, if he needs help, the IRA's a fair possibility. They'd help him, all right; they rely a lot on the money the SS give them. The girl has only just appeared on the scene and Lockhart is in a vulnerable position as regards blackmail. So if she's in the IRA and working with Vogel . . ." His voice tailed off.

"A lot of ifs," Anton observed.

"Do you have any better ideas?" Paul asked, mildly.

Tyler set aside the folder and stretched his arms, aware of a slight cramp in his back. Getting out of condition, he thought; too much sitting at desks, that's what it is.

The folders contained details of the four men that had been placed under surveillance. Four minutely detailed biographies, only lacking in one aspect; which of them had sold out to the Germans. A further thought struck him: was this really going to help him find the German agents? Or was it, as he privately thought, an irrelevant sideline?

Randall finished reading the last of the four files and looked up. "A tough one, sir."

"You're not kidding. Any thoughts?"

"Well, none of them really stand out as possibilities. They all seem whiter than white to me."

"But one of them is a traitor. Which one, though?" mused Tyler, half to himself. He looked at Randall. "Let's be honest, if there was anything incriminating in these files, it would have been picked up long ago. So we'll just have to go through each man's life with a fine tooth comb. Bank accounts, families, friends, mistresses, the lot. We'll have to tap their telephones and put them all under twenty four hour surveillance. Anybody they talk to will be investigated, even if it's only the postman. The works, in fact."

Randall whistled. "It could take months."

"Probably will, but we've got our orders, so we'll just have to get on with it, won't we?"

Despite his words, Tyler shared Randall's pessimism. He was quite sure that whoever had landed at Markyate and Aldeburgh would not be waiting long before carrying out their operation. He had the distinct feeling that they were being led away from the scent by this investigation, that while they were following these four men around, the Germans would strike. And whatever they planned to do, it was going to be big; of that he was certain.

Tyler was a conscientious man; he did not like to leave things uncompleted and he had the distinct feeling that he was missing something, that the whole situation just didn't quite add up. Or, rather, he knew what didn't add up: the separate arrivals in Hertfordshire and Suffolk, but he could not fathom out why they had chosen to do things that way. He had a gnawing feeling that the two incidents were important, that if he could find out why they had taken place, he would be a large step closer to unravelling the mystery.

Trouble is, he thought, nobody else seems to attach much importance to it.

He picked up one of the folders at random. He opened it

and studied the photograph on the first page. Are you our traitor, my friend?

Although he had no way of knowing it, the photograph in front of him was that of the man Paul knew as 'Jaguar'.

BERLIN.

"Your coat, Herr Admiral," said the orderly.

Canaris grunted an acknowledgement as he put on the coat that was being held up for him and then turned to face Keitel. "Thank you for the excellent dinner, Herr General."

"My pleasure, Canaris," said Keitel, clasping the proferred hand. "You must come again soon."

"I'll do my best," Canaris replied, although the prospect appalled him; even though Keitel was head of the German High Command, Canaris regarded him as little more than an imbecile. On the other hand, Canaris reflected, he was a useful friend to have, as he was known to be slavishly devoted to Hitler . . . And had it not been for Keitel's intervention, Canaris knew that he would probably have been arrested by the Gestapo by now. These occasional "bull sessions" were a small price to pay for such protection, even if they were indescribably boring; Canaris had made his excuses as soon as he decently could.

He completed the farewells at the front door and then went down the steps to where his car was waiting. He nodded distantly to Baumann, his driver; he was preoccupied. He was expecting a message from 'Angel', his contact in the SS headquarters in Prinzalbrechtstrasse. He had no idea how 'Angel' would deliver the message, only that it would be important.

Canaris sat back in the seat as the car pulled away and reached into his coat pocket for one of his cigars. His fingers encountered a piece of folded up paper; it had certainly not been there when he had arrived at Keitel's house. He smiled appreciatively; how the devil had 'Angel' managed that?

He glanced at Baumann and then took out the sheet of paper. He switched on the interior light, smoothed out the paper and began to read.

"My God," he murmured. He read the message a second time and then stared unseeingly out of the window. This was even worse than they'd thought! The prospect of someone like Churchill being killed had been bad enough, but this was far worse . . . He sighed; they really had no alternative any longer. The British would have to be informed. Doing so would place Koenig and Lorenz in greater danger, of course, but there was nothing else for it. In the final analysis, they were expendable . . . But 'Faust' was not.

He looked at the message a third time. 'Angel' had been right, he reflected; the message had indeed been important. How 'Angel' had done it, Canaris had no idea; but he had discovered Faust's true identity.

Vogel and Roeder had been sent to England to kill His Majesty King George the Sixth.

CHAPTER 5

LONDON.

Tyler arrived at Fenton's office at five minutes to ten, wondering why he had been summoned so urgently. Fenton had telephoned him at home but without giving any hints as to what was afoot; but there again, Tyler reflected, he wouldn't over the phone.

"Ah, Tyler, good of you to be so prompt."

Tyler sat down, thinking to himself that it had better be urgent; he had been working until four in the morning and had only managed about three hours sleep before Fenton's call. He wondered if Fenton would take ages to come to the point; he usually did.

Today, however, was different, which immediately indicated how urgent the matter was. "There's been a rather extraordinary development in connection with these German agents we're looking for."

"Really?"

"Yes. We have received a message directly from Abwehr HQ.' Fenton paused, theatrically.

The gesture was wasted on Tyler. "Look, sir, I must be a bit thick this morning. You mean they just sent us a direct message?"

"That is precisely what I mean. A direct communication through the Geneva conduit using one of our own codes. To be perfectly frank, we did not even know it had been broken."

"You're satisfied it's genuine?"

"We believe so. The contents of the message are so important that we cannot afford to assume otherwise."

68

"Are you going to tell me what the message is, or do I have to guess it?"

Fenton did not look in the least put out by Tyler's peevish outburst. "There is, apparently, a two man SS group in London at the moment. Their mission," again, Fenton paused for dramatic effect, "is to assassinate the King."

"My God," whispered Tyler, both awestruck and appalled.

"So you see why we cannot afford to ignore it."

"But why are they telling us?"

"Apparently, according to the message, there are a large number of high ranking Wehrmacht officers who are opposed to Hitler's regime and are trying to get rid of him so that they can negotiate a peace treaty with ourselves and the Americans. Russia does not come into their plans, so it seems. This group feel, not unreasonably, that the assassination of His Majesty would not exactly make us too keen on this idea and so they wish to prevent it happening."

Tyler stared in disbelief; not so much at what Fenton was saying, but at the casual, offhand way he was saying it. It was hardly a joking matter, after all. Didn't Fenton care? Just then, it occurred to Tyler that Fenton's flippancy, which was unusual for him, might be a way of concealing his true feelings. "I see," said Tyler. "Does this Anti-Hitler group exist, or is it a hoax?"

"According to the OSS, yes. Their man, Dulles, in Geneva, has had several contacts with them. I have also had it confirmed from—shall we say—higher authority."

Which meant Cabinet level, in all probability, thought Tyler. "So this group has warned us, then?"

"Yes. They've given us as complete a dossier on the assassination squad as they can, they say."

Tyler relaxed slightly at the hint of scepticism in Fenton's voice. This was more like the Fenton he knew.

"It's under the command of a Karl Vogel. The other man is named Roeder. Vogel's apparently one of their top line undercover operatives, while Roeder is a rifle marksman. They've given us full descriptions of both men but they haven't given us any information as to when and how the assassination is to take place. Still, at least we know who we're looking for."

Fenton pushed a file across the desk, which Tyler glanced through. He looked up. "This only mentions two men. We know two men landed in Hertfordshire, so who landed in Suffolk? Why haven't they mentioned them?"

"A good point," Fenton agreed. "Unless only one man landed in Hertfordshire but left two parachutes to mislead us."

"Bit devious, isn't it? Maybe it was Roeder who killed Gilmore but I honestly can't see the logic in sending in the two men separately. I'd say there's a second group and they haven't told us anything about them."

"You think the Hertfordshire group could be a decoy? That the Suffolk group is the real assassination squad?"

"It's possible, sir. While we're looking for Vogel and Roeder, the Suffolk group could be carrying out their operation."

Fenton considered this and it was evident from his face that he did not like the notion at all. "I'm afraid you could well be right. Except—why tell us the target?"

"Perhaps he isn't the target at all. Perhaps that's a decoy as well."

"You could be right," Fenton admitted, glumly. "The trouble is, we can't afford to ignore it. All we can do is to take steps to protect His Majesty then to try and find Vogel as well as this second group, about which we know nothing."

Both men were silent for a while as they considered the enormity of the situation. My God, thought Tyler again. I wonder if he feels as scared as I do? They could be anywhere, for God's sake. They could strike tomorrow, or in three months time, in London, or Windsor, or Balmoral. There weren't even any pictures, only descriptions, which might be accurate or deliberately misleading. And they might not even be after the King at all; any of the Royal Family would do equally as well for a propaganda victory.

The main question, really, was this; could Vogel do it?

Very possibly, thought Tyler, as he read the dossier. The

King wouldn't be that difficult to kill. He believed in being seen by the public as much as possible.

"Can we persuade the King to leave London?"

"It is going to be suggested to him by the Prime Minister himself, but we are not optimistic. Winston was fairly certain that his reply would be No, that his place is with his people. Remember that he refused to leave the Palace during the Blitz. An admirable attitude, of course, but hardly helpful to us."

"But we will be taking extra security measures?"

"Of course." He looked at Tyler. "In the meantime your job, Tyler, is still to find Vogel and this second group."

"And when I find them?"

"Just remember that the King's safety is paramount. You may use whatever measures are necessary to safeguard His Majesty."

Tyler nodded heavily. "So, if I put in requests for firearms?"

"They will be approved, without question."

Tyler looked again at the dossier. Somehow, he didn't think the German agents would give up without a fight; it would come to a shoot-out if they ever found them.

If.

"Cup of tea, sir?"

Tyler did not move. The typist waited a few seconds and then repeated her question. Tyler looked up, startled. "Pardon?"

"Cup of tea, sir." She held out the cup and saucer.

"Oh—yes, thank you." He put the cup on the desk as she left. The folder Fenton had given him lay on the desk next to the cup; he almost knew its contents by heart but was still no nearer to finding Vogel than before. Randall had circulated the descriptions to Scotland Yard but they had not been very optimistic. The details could fit anybody . . . short of interrogating everyone who matched the descriptions, there was not very much that could be done.

Tyler ignored the tea. If I were in Vogel's position, what would I do? he wondered. He would contact a local agent, in all probability, but there were no known German agents in London, only the unidentified source in the Home Office. Each of the four suspects were under surveillance but nothing had turned up so far. In any case, there was no guarantee that Vogel did not have another contact, about whom M15 knew nothing.

One of Tyler's first steps had been to find out who had access to the sort of information Vogel would need, especially the King's itineraries. Each of these potential contacts were also under observation but there had been no developments. In any case, the information was not that difficult to come by; it was available to anybody with a press pass, for example. The Press were generally notified twenty-four hours in advance of public engagements by the King, so that they would be given proper coverage; all Vogel needed was to suborn a reporter and so a number of journalists were under surveillance as well.

In short, Tyler reflected, a lot of people were being followed around London with no results at all yet. There was also the very real possibility that Vogel already had all the information he needed; and if this was so, all of their precautions would be futile. It would also mean that he could strike at any time . . .

He turned round at a knock at the door. "Come in."

It was Randall. He had asked him to start checking their four suspects to see which of them would have access to the itineraries.

"Well?"

"Two of them have been ruled out—Lucas and Snell. Neither of them have access."

"Good. We'll concentrate on the other two, Porter and—" he hesitated; to his annoyance, the other man's name had slipped his mind.

"Harcourt," Randall reminded him.

"Harcourt, Yes. We'll keep a token watch on Lucas and Snell, just in case. No luck with the descriptions?"

"Several false alarms but that's all. Trouble is, we waste a lot of time checking them out."

"I know but we'll just have to take the time."

Tyler seemed to notice the cup of tea for the first time. He took a sip and grimaced. It was cold.

"Menzies' department—they're being watched?" he continued.

"Yes. All of them and their associates."

"Anything?"

"Only some probably harmless scandals. Menzies has a mistress and Lockhart looks as though he's being unfaithful to his fiancée. We're watching both of them, but—"

"Yes, I know. Nothing," Tyler finished for him. "Just remember, these scandals could be useful for blackmail."

"Or they could be completely harmless."

"Yes, I know that too." He shook his head in despair. Vogel could be anywhere and all they were doing was to probe into the private lives of people who were probably innocent. And what if there was a second group?

I don't think we're going to find them in time, he thought, with a sudden chill.

Paul was perturbed. He had just received word from Anton that Lockhart was under surveillance; he had been followed to Maureen's flat the night before and the tail had gone with him when he left. As far as he could say, nobody was watching the girl but he could not be one hundred per cent certain of that.

Which posed an important question. Why were the British keeping a low level clerk under surveillance? Obviously, Lockhart was under suspicion—of being an Abwehr agent, perhaps? It probably had no connection with their own operation but it meant that they would have to be careful in their surveillance.

He stopped dead in his tracks. Supposing there was a connection? Lockhart, after all, had access to the sort of data that Vogel would need. What if the British were watching

Lockhart for the same reason he was? That meant that they would have to know about Vogel's mission—yet how could they? Just what was going on?

Paul had reached the Marriott's house. He went in and slowly climbed the stairs. He felt very tense and hesitant. If the British knew about the assassination plot, then they would be pulling out all the stops; and if any of his own group were captured, they would assume they were with Vogel. Perhaps he ought to pull out; the situation was becoming increasingly hazardous. If either Anton or himself were captured and the British thought they were intending to assassinate Churchill then the British would not bother with the Geneva Convention . . . perhaps they should pull out . . .

Paul opened his room door and went in.

He froze.

Somebody was in the bed. As soon as the thought registered, he realised who it was and relaxed. He turned on the light.

Carolyn lay in the bed, the blankets pulled up to her chin. She looked at him, half fearfully, half excitedly.

"Hallo, Carolyn," said Paul, gently. "What's going on?"

"I'm trying to seduce you," she replied, smiling mischievously. "Mum and Dad are at my aunt's and they won't be back at all tonight. They think I'm staying with a friend of mine from work. I'd rather stay with you, though."

Paul closed the door and went to the bed. He sat on the edge, looking down at her, his face showing none of the confusion he felt. He'd be a bloody fool if he took her up on it. On the other hand, he told himself, she was undeniably attractive. It would also ease the tension that he could feel within him. Supposing he refused—"Hell hath no fury" and so on; he might have to find other lodgings.

He smiled wryly. Stop rationalising, he told himself; you want her, so why not?

As if reading his mind, she pulled the covers down to reveal her breasts. Reluctantly, his eyes returned to her face, to her moist, slightly parted lips. He leaned forward and kissed her, his hand gently caressing her firm breast.

He drew away and undressed, quickly. He went to turn off the light.

"No, leave it on," she said quietly. "I want to see you. And I want you to see me." Her voice was husky, tremulous.

He went back to the bed. Slowly, he pulled back the blankets, exposing her slim, naked body. He lay down beside her and took her in his arms, his mouth pressing urgently against hers as she surrendered herself to him. Slowly, gently, they made love until their mingled passion surged and flowed like the waves breaking on the shore leaving them spent and at peace.

"You must think I'm a right little tart," Carolyn said. She was lying with her head on Paul's chest, feeling drowsily relaxed. Before he could answer, she went on, "Don't say anything. I'll try to explain.

"It's the War, Paul. Everything's so uncertain. You can't take anything for granted. We could all be dead tomorrow. Supposing I hadn't seduced you tonight and one of us was killed by a doodlebug tomorrow? I'd have missed out on this. I'd never have known what it was like with you. Do you see what I'm getting at?"

"I think I do," said Paul, softly.

"I'm not sure you do. Have you ever heard of Wilfred Owen?"

"The poet? Yes." He had been right; she was a lot more intelligent than he had first thought.

"He was killed only a week before the Armistice in the last war. Did you know that? Suppose he had decided to wait until the war was over before writing his poems? They would all have been lost. We have to make every second count, Paul. We can't afford to waste time. I wanted you to make love to me. I could see you wanted me but you weren't sure about it so I thought, why waste time?"

Paul looked up at the ceiling, remembering. Ilse. Long dark hair, blue eyes. Tall, slender, with skin like alabaster, except that where alabaster was cold, her body was warm, vibrant. Why waste time . . . suddenly, he knew why Carolyn was so obsessed by war's uncertainty.

"Did you love him very much?"

Startled, she stared at him and then relaxed. "We were engaged," she said quietly. "I'd known him for years—we grew up together. Oh, he'd been out with other girls before me but I was the first he went steady with. He was a couple of years older than me.

"We'd been going out together for about six months when he was called up. He went into the Navy, back in 1940. He got a shore posting at Sheerness so we weren't very worried. We were dead lucky, really—he was home every third weekend.

"We got engaged at Christmas and planned to get married at the end of May. We weren't in any real hurry, you see. We didn't want to rush into it—we wanted it all to be just right. We didn't even go to bed together because we wanted to wait until the wedding night." She fell silent for a while, remembering. "We must have been mad," she said, at length.

"Anyway, May came round. We were all starting to get ready for the Big Day when the Admiralty dropped a bombshell on us. He was given a sea posting and was ordered to report to his ship a week before the wedding. We had to postpone it, of course—there wasn't time to post the banns if we'd brought it forward.

"The night before he left, we went to bed together. We were both frightened by what might happen to him so we decided not to wait for the wedding. We were in bed, stark naked, trying to relax so we could start, when the air raid sirens went. We almost stayed where we were, but we didn't, so that when he left the next day, I was still a virgin.

"He told me not to worry, because he was joining the most powerful warship in the Royal Navy, so he was safe as houses. He went off up to Scotland to join her and she sailed two days later to chase the *Bismarck*. He was on the *Hood*."

Paul said nothing.

"There were only three survivors. He wasn't one of them."

She was silent for a full minute. Then, she seemed to collect herself.

"We never even had sex, Paul—because we waited. I'll never know what it would have been like and that's the worst part, not knowing." Once again, she fell silent for a few moments and then, with a visible effort, she brightened.

"I'm sorry, Paul. I shouldn't have rambled on like that."

"It's alright," he said.

"Thank you for listening. I've never told anyone about it before. I just wanted you to know why I was so—well—forward."

"I can see why you were," he said, softly, touching her cheek. He grinned, mischievously. "Mind you, I'm not complaining."

They kissed, gently at first, then with increasing passion. Neither of them said anything for quite some time after that.

Paul lay awake after she had gone to sleep, staring up at the ceiling. Remembering things that were perhaps best forgotten. Only, he knew he never would, never could.

Ilse. Ilse Lehmann. The girl next door. They had gone to school together, had even been in the same class. He had walked with her to and from school until they had reached that age where girls were "cissies" and boys were "silly" and then they had studiously ignored each other, not wanting to be teased by their friends.

Paul could still recall when he suddenly realised that Ilse wasn't a little tomboy any more but an attractive girl, with a figure that was becoming increasingly noticeable.

He could also recall how jealous he had been of Georg Meissner when he had taken her to the Christmas Dance in Sassnitz. His own turn came soon after, when he and Ilse started to "go steady". Gradually, the relationship became more intimate, the rather timid early kisses giving way to longer, more passionate embraces, until, one glorious summer's day in the sand dunes east of Sassnitz, they had become lovers.

Almost before it had begun, their relationship was brought to an end. Paul's parents decided to leave Germany. His father was an outspoken critic of the Nazis and he no longer felt safe once they had come to power. The family had left for England in August, 1933. Ilse had been in tears when they parted.

They had written to each other every week at first, letters that grew progressively more explicit and longing, until Paul, by now at Oxford, was seduced by the bored wife of one of the lecturers. He had been twenty; she had been twelve years older. Almost overnight, she made Paul realise just how inexperienced he was. His letters to Ilse became less torrid, although hers remained almost pornographic for some months, until, he surmised, she too had found someone else. After this, the letters decreased in frequency as well as in eroticism, although they kept in touch until 1938, when Ilse wrote that she was engaged to an army officer. The correspondence stopped completely then.

At Oxford, Paul became fluent in English but wanted to return to Germany—he could still remember the heated arguments between himself and his father. As far as Paul was concerned, National Socialism had brought prosperity and peace to his homeland; he had dismissed the stories of Jews being persecuted as being Communist propaganda. Germany was becoming a great nation once again and he wanted to share in its success . . .

Then had come the shattering news of the car crash that killed both of his parents. Once he began to think clearly again, Paul realised that there was nothing to keep him in England and so he returned to Germany to share in the new prosperity. Later, disillusionment had set in.

He was approached almost immediately by the Abwehr, firstly to answer questions about Britain but within three months he had been recruited as an Abwehr agent.

He went back to Sassnitz to discover that Ilse was married and living in Berlin. With only a hint of regret that he acknowledged was probably nostalgia, he decided to forget her. He had done so, until the autumn of 1942, when they met, quite by chance, in a Berlin restaurant.

Ilse was then twenty-eight years old and an undeniably beautiful woman. He soon discovered that she was a widow— her husband had been killed during the first week of the Russian Campaign the previous year.

They had gone back to the flat she shared with another girl—providentially away for the weekend—and were in bed only minutes after that. The frenzied urgency of the first time gave way to a slower, gentler exploration as they re-discovered each other. As they both agreed, each of them had learned a lot since 1933 . . . The weeks slipped past in a delicious euphoria. They made utopian plans, as lovers do; they would marry, buy a chateau in the Bavarian Alps, spend all day in bed, forget the war, forget the world . . .

But the world had not allowed them to forget for long.

Paul clenched his teeth, driving his memories away. He turned over and looked at Carolyn sleeping beside him. You're wrong, love, he thought. You say it's terrible not to know what it would have been like with your fiancé but you can't miss something you never had. It's far worse to know how wonderful it can be and to know that it's never going to happen again, ever . . .

Lockhart returned home at just after midnight. The evening had been a disaster. He and Claire had gone to dinner with her brother and his wife, but he had been morose and preoccupied. Claire had complained to him about his unsociable behaviour on the way back to her house in the taxi; not for the first time, the prospect of married life with her sent a chill down his spine. She was becoming increasingly shrewish, these days . . . He had made the excuse that he was rushed off his feet at the office trying to ensure that everything would be neat and tidy for when he left to take up his new appointment. She had been at least partly mollified by the time they arrived at her house but the real reason for his preoccupation had still been preying on his mind.

Maureen Riordan: what was he to do about her? He had been on tenterhooks ever since that encounter outside the pub on their second date with that fellow from the Home Office. Despite the risk, however, Lockhart had continued to see Maureen; he could not give her up, not yet, not while his visits to her flat were so . . . uninhibited. And yet it would have to come to an end . . .

He was still keep in thought as he opened the door to his flat and went in. He was half aware of a movement behind him and then he felt a searing pain in the back of his head.

Slowly, painfully, he regained consciousness. He was in

darkness; he noticed this before he realised that he was tied very securely to a chair.

"What's going on?" he called out, fearfully.

As if waiting for the cue, a light came on behind him. Automatically, he started to turn around . . .

"Don't." The command was abrupt—and from behind him. Lockhart looked ahead of him, suddenly aware of the trembling in his stomach. This couldn't be happening—he was still in his own living room! Dear God, he was being held prisoner in his own flat . . .

"Who are you? What do you want?" he said, his voice no more than a croak. The trembling in his gut had spread to his limbs now.

Abruptly, something was held in front of his face. It was several seconds before he realised it was a photograph. It was still longer before the picture came into focus. Lockhart gasped. It couldn't be! The naked girl was—was Maureen! And the man with her was . . .

No! He closed his eyes. No. It couldn't be.

"You recognise them?" said the voice from behind him.

"What do you want?" Lockhart asked, dully. "Money? I don't have much, but you can have it all."

"No, not money. Co-operation." There was a pause.

"What do you mean?" said Lockhart when he could stand the silence no longer.

"I want you to photograph something for me. A document."

"A document? You're a spy!"

There was no answer.

"A spy!" Lockhart repeated. He took a deep breath. "No. I won't do it."

Another photograph was held in front of him. And another; if anything, each one was worse than the last.

"Just one document, that's all, then you can have those photographs. That's all it will need."

Lockhart stared mesmerised at the pictures as they were held in front of him, one by one.

80

"I'm sure I can think of several people who would be very interested in these," the voice continued. "Your department head, perhaps? No. I think Sir Charles Hamilton would be better. And his daughter, of course. I doubt very much that there would be any marriage once they see these. And if there is no marriage then what price your promotion? Or your career, come to that. By the time Sir Charles has finished with you, Lockhart, you wouldn't even get a job on a dustcart."

"You're—you're bluffing!"

"Do you really want to take that risk, Lockhart? It's quite simple. Do as I ask and you'll get these photographs and their negatives. Your marriage to Miss Hamilton will take place and your future will be assured. Refuse and you will be ruined. I am not bluffing."

Lockhart stared hopelessly at the photographs for almost half a minute and then nodded in defeat. "All right," he said dully. "I don't really have any choice, do I?"

"No, you don't." The photographs were removed. "I'm glad you've decided to see sense. In a moment, you will be given an injection that will put you to sleep. When you awake, you'll find a small camera, as well as these photographs. You can dispose of them however you like but remember that there are others, each of them as—interesting—as these. In any case, I still have the negatives. You will take the camera to your office tomorrow and photograph certain documents. I want copies of the VIP Itineraries for the next month, complete copies. Is this clear?"

"Why do you want them?"

The voice ignored him. "If you fail to provide me with these copies or if you attempt to substitute another document, or you do not provide a complete copy, or you tell anyone else what has happened, then I will send the photographs to Sir Charles. Is all this clear?"

"Yes! Yes! I said I'd do it!"

"Good. Bring the camera, with the film still inside, of course, back to your flat tomorrow evening. I shall then contact you to make arrangements for collection. Once I have verified that you have fully obeyed your instructions the remaining photographs and negatives will be returned to you. Not before. Understand?"

"Yes," whispered Lockhart. Suddenly, a blinding light shone full in his eyes and, simultaneously, he felt a stinging pain in his left wrist. The pain died away, the light faded . . .

Vogel nodded to himself in satisfaction. He felt sure that Lockhart would do exactly as he was told. The only thing that worried him was that it had looked as though Lockhart was under surveillance; someone had been following him along the street. Vogel had watched from Lockhart's window as the tail had taken up position in the shadows opposite the flat. After he had dealt with Lockhart, Vogel had crossed to the window again; the tail was still there. After ten minutes or so, Vogel had turned off the lights as though Lockhart were going to bed: the tail had immediately walked off along the street.

Lockhart was under observation, obviously, but it was very low-key. The flat was not being watched; the tail was only following Lockhart himself and he had left once he assumed Lockhart had gone to bed. The surveillance made things a little more difficult. If they were watching Lockhart, they would almost certainly know about Maureen by now; he would have to be careful in dealing with both of them, when the time came.

Anton telephoned the contact's number and gave the code identification.

"Any news?" he asked.

"Only from Jaguar. He says he has an urgent message for Keen."

"Does Keen know about this?"

"No. He's not due to call in until tomorrow, unless anything turns up."

"What does Jaguar want?"

"A meeting, usual place, but at one this afternoon."

"I see. I'd better go instead. If Keen does phone in, tell him that I'll meet Jaguar."

"I'll do that."

Anton rang off. What did Jaguar want? He knew dam' well that he had to give at least twenty four hours notice of a proposed rendezvous. It sounded serious—so urgent that it couldn't wait. If so, then the rendezvous had to be kept and Anton would have to keep it.

God help him if it wasn't important, thought Anton.

"These are the documents you requested, Mr Lockhart," said Miss Waters.

Lockhart jumped as if stung. "Eh? Er, pardon?"

The typist stared curiously at him. "Are you all right, Mr Lockhart?"

"Yes, fine. You startled me, that's all. Are these the documents I sent for?"

"Yes, that's what I said."

"I'm sorry." He forced a smile with an effort. "I was miles away, I'm afraid."

"So I gathered." She placed the pile of documents on his desk.

"Thank you, Miss Waters."

She gave him a frosty smile as she left.

Lockhart stared unseeingly at the papers. He was shaking uncontrollably. He had to pull himself together! He had already drawn attention to himself too many times this morning with his pale, strained face. A thousand times he had asked himself how he had ever got into this mess. How could he have been so stupid? Why hadn't he realised that she had only been using him for her own ends? Because she must have known what was happening . . .

He looked up at the clock. 1.15. Everyone would be out to lunch. Unsteadily, he went to the door and locked it. He took the camera from his briefcase and set it on the desk.

He sorted through the documents until he found the VIP Itineraries. He picked up the camera and then hesitated. He could still back out. Report it to the police, let them set a trap.

Lockhart shook his head in despair. The voice had warned him what would happen if he did not co-operate and he believed it.

He had no alternative.

83

Lockhart began to photograph the documents, somehow remembering the typed instructions that had been left with the camera. Six sheets, one frame for each. It took less than a minute. Hurriedly, he replaced the documents in the pile, returned the camera to his briefcase and sat down.

Then, the trembling returned, an uncontrollable fit that left him exhausted and drenched in perspiration.

Randall watched Harcourt as the other man threw breadcrumbs to the ducks in the Serpentine. This was an invariable routine in Harcourt's lunch hour and so far there had been no change in the established pattern. Randall had positioned himself about thirty yards from Harcourt, apparently engaged in earnest conversation with his girlfriend; she was, in fact, Tyler's secretary, brought along as cover. Randall was now so sure of Harcourt's habits that he had sent the girl along first so that he could "meet" her at the same bench at the same time; a regular lunchtime date, if anyone happened to be watching.

Harcourt was sure he was not being followed; he had checked several times. In any case, there was no reason to believe he was under surveillance. He half-noticed the courting couple on their usual bench as well as the family gathering about twenty yards along the water's edge. No-one seemed to be watching him; it was safe for him to meet 'Keen'.

Anton recognised Harcourt from Paul's description; he had been told that 'Jaguar' would be feeding the ducks. Anton went and stood next to Harcourt; he began to toss his own breadcrumbs into the water. Harcourt glanced at him.

"They seem to be rather more keen on your bread," said Anton, emphasising the word 'keen'.

Harcourt nodded as he recognised the reference to Paul's cover name. "Where is he?" he asked, in a low voice.

"Couldn't get here. But he sends his best regards and asks to be mentioned to the Admiral."

Harcourt relaxed at the code introduction. "Very well. I'll get straight to the point. M15 know about Vogel."

Anton said nothing for a few moments. As far as he knew, Jaguar knew nothing about Vogel but he was no fool; he had connected Vogel's mission with their own. "How?"

"I don't know but they have a complete dossier on him and his group. There's a full scale search on for him. Is he anything to do with you?"

"Not directly, no."

"But the search could make things difficult for you?"

"Possibly, yes," Anton replied, guardedly. "And you have no idea how they acquired this information?"

"Not definitely. Judging by its detail, though, it's almost as if it were taken directly from Abwehr or SS files. It's got just about everything, heights, ages, descriptions, the lot, even their names."

Anton thought for a moment. "Was there any indication as to what they're planning to do?"

Harcourt shook his head. "No. The documents I saw were M15's, that had been prepared for distribution. They just contained details of the men they were looking for."

"When did they get the information?"

"I don't know. I saw it this morning."

"Very well, I'll let Keen know. Anything else?"

"No."

"Very well. Cheerio," Anton said casually and wandered away. He was much more worried than he looked. How the devil had M15 obtained a complete dossier on Vogel and Roeder? Obviously, they had someone very high up in either the Abwehr or the SS; either way, it meant trouble. To have the entire British security alerted and searching for a German undercover group was the last thing they wanted.

In his preoccupation, Anton did not notice Randall get up from the bench behind him, nor did he observe the signal he made.

Randall had observed Harcourt talking to a man he had never seen before, but whose description loosely matched Vogel's. He would have to be questioned; it was probably yet another false lead but it had to be followed.

A uniformed policeman stopped Anton at the gate. "Excuse me, sir. May I see your identification, please?"

Anton looked up, taken aback. "Er—pardon?"

"Your identification papers, sir. Just a routine check."

"Oh—er, certainly, constable," said Anton, not unduly concerned as he handed over the documents; he had been subjected to two spot checks in the last few days. It was only when Randall came up that he began to worry; he recognised him as one of the courting couple by the Serpentine. The constable handed the papers to Randall and then Anton understood. This was no random spot check. Harcourt had been under surveillance and so now he, Anton, was under suspicion.

Randall looked unconcernedly at Anton. "Name?"

"Antony Lawrence."

"Date of birth?"

"7th of August, 1913. Look—"

"Later, sir. Just a routine enquiry. Do you know Mr Harcourt well?"

"Who?"

"You were talking to him just now."

"Oh, him! No, I don't know him, not by name. I sometimes see him when I feed the ducks, that's all."

"I see. How often do you come here, Mr Lawrence?"

"Not very often. Generally at weekends, or on my day off."

"It says here that you live in Leytonstone."

"Yes. Kirby Gardens."

"Why did you come here today, then?"

Anton was very perturbed now. He was being asked to reveal too many details of his supposed existence. "No particular reason."

"You came all the way from Leytonstone just to feed the ducks?"

"I was visiting someone."

"I see. Could I ask who?"

"Look, just what is this?"

"We'd appreciate your help, sir. Who were you visiting?"

"My girlfriend."

"Could you give me her name and address, sir?"

"I'd rather not say."

"Why not?"

"Well—" He hesitated. "She's married." There was a hint of conspiracy in his voice.

"I see."

There was nothing he could put his finger on, but Randall was suspicious. His reason for not wanting to name who he was visiting—genuine? It was certainly plausible enough but was he trying not to give any details that could be checked? And why waste time by the Serpentine when he was on his way to a clandestine meeting with a married woman?

"May I see your wallet, sir?"

"But why—"

"Please, sir," said Randall, firmly.

Anton felt it was time for a touch of impatience. "Look, I'd like to know what is going on."

"I could explain it all to you down at the local police station if you'd prefer, sir."

Resignedly, Anton handed over the wallet. Randall thumbed through it and took out a small photograph of an attractive young woman with blonde hair.

"Is this your lady friend, sir?"

"Yes," Anton muttered.

Randall turned it over and read the message on the back: "All my love—Diana." Not exactly helpful, he reflected.

Abruptly, he came to a decision. "Would you come with me, please, sir?"

"Where to?"

"The police station. We think you can help us with some inquiries we're making."

Suddenly, Anton was aware of four men surrounding him. He could probably deal with two of them, maybe even three but it was useless to take on four. He relaxed, imperceptibly;

87

even Randall, who was watching for it, missed his reaction and saw only indignation.

"Very well. If you insist." He really had no choice. Perhaps he could make a run for it on the way. If the worst came to the worst, he might just be able to bluff it out.

Somehow, he doubted it . . .

CHAPTER 6

Tyler threw down the stack of reports in disgust. There had been no positive results at all from the surveillance so far. He had absolutely nothing to give Fenton, who was becoming increasingly impatient. It was quite possible that he would take over the manhunt himself; Tyler had mixed feelings about that.

The phone rang. "Yes?"

"Randall here, sir. I'm questioning a man who fits Vogel's description. He spoke to Harcourt. I've got—well, just a feeling about him."

"Why?"

"Nothing I can put a finger on. He's evasive, for one thing. He doesn't seem to want to reveal anything that isn't on his papers. Says he's going to meet a married woman but takes time to feed the ducks and talk to Harcourt. Calls the woman his 'girlfriend'. If you were having it away with a married bit, would you call her a girlfriend?"

"I might," said Tyler, drily. "Depends what she looks like. It's a bit flimsy, isn't it, though?"

"I know. I just have this hunch. I thought you might like to have a word with him."

Tyler was tempted to tell him what to do with his hunch but thought better of it. Randall was a good, thorough investigator and wouldn't have phoned unless he felt he was on to something. In any case, there was damn all else to go on . . .

"Right, I'll come over. Whereabouts are you?"

Anton stared morosely at the wall, thinking furiously. It was fairly easy to figure out what had happened. 'Jaguar' had been "blown" and had been under surveillance. Anton, therefore, had placed himself in jeopardy by contacting him. Just how dangerous the situation was depended on how suspicious they were of him. His cover would not stand up to a really close scrutiny. His papers described him as an independent travelling salesman so that there were no employers to check with. However, a deeper probe would blow it apart. They would find a suitcase full of brushes but no customers; once they started delving into his fictitious background they would soon know he was not who he claimed to be.

Not for the first time, he cursed the hurried way in which the operation had been mounted; not that he blamed Paul, or anyone else, for that matter. There had been no time to devise really deep covers but that was scant comfort now.

The door of his cell opened and two men walked in. One was the tall, thin man who had already questioned him, but Anton took careful note of the other one, who was even taller and broader. He looked as though he were more used to hand to hand combat than interrogation. Anton wondered if he was the British equivalent of the Gestapo thugs who beat their victims into submission, but a look at the shrewd, intelligent eyes made him doubt this.

"Mr Lawrence, isn't it? My name's Tyler. I'd like to clear up some problems that have arisen." His tone was very polite, courteous. "You see, we're looking for a man who fits your description."

"I see," said Anton, almost tempted to believe him.

"You live at 48, Kirby Gardens, Leytonstone?"

"I have digs there. With Mrs Fuller."

"For how long?"

"I've been there for three weeks."

"And before that?"

"Pardon?" This was the first rule of interrogation; don't answer any question until you have to.

"Where were you living before that?"

Anton now answered without hesitation; he had thought

out his answer already. "Walthamstow. Cedar Road, Number 22."

The thin man made a careful note. Anton watched Tyler, waiting for the serious questions to start. They couldn't do much with that address; it had been totally destroyed by a V1 flying bomb two weeks ago. He had seen it. The adjoining houses had been gutted; they would find it difficult to prove he had never lived there. He remembered the name of the family—it had been mentioned by a neighbour, one of a small group watching the ARP wardens picking their way gingerly through the rubble. "With the Greens."

"How long did you live there, Mr Lawrence?"

"About six or seven months."

"Good. Now, it says on your papers that you are exempt from military duties on the grounds of a weak heart."

"Yes." This was dangerous.

"Would you object to being given a medical examination?"

"Would you mind telling me why?" Anton's voice did not betray the cold feeling he had in the pit of his stomach. There was no way that he could bluff his way through a medical; he was in A1 physical condition.

"We're trying to prove you're who you say you are, Mr Lawrence."

"And who am I supposed to be?"

Tyler's voice changed abruptly. "It's not who you are, it's what you're planning to do, Vogel."

Anton looked confused, nothing more. "What did you call me? That's not my name."

Tyler did not answer. He wanted to give the other man time for the implications to sink in, to let Vogel—if it was Vogel—know that he knew his real identity.

Anton's face still showed nothing more than bewilderment but he knew that he had lost. If they believed he was Vogel, they would investigate his cover. They would penetrate it and then they would really start on him. They would not feel bound by the Geneva Convention, for which he could hardly blame them. In their position, he would not have any qualms about beating the truth out of a suspected assassin. The interrogation would be ruthless and, in time, he would either talk or go insane. With a skilled interrogator, it would be the former.

An agent under questioning withholds information for various reasons. One is loyalty to one's country, although this loses its power the longer the interrogation goes on. It may be pride, the sense of self-respect, in that he wants to make it as difficult as possible for his captors. It may be to protect the other members of his group, give them time to escape; the longer he held out, the better their chances.

The trouble was, thought Anton, he could only betray Paul, not Vogel. If he told them the truth, they were hardly likely to believe him. So, for Paul's sake, he had to hold out as long as possible to give Paul a chance to get out.

"My name isn't Vogel, it's Lawrence."

Tyler stared thoughtfully at the prisoner. If he was Vogel, it looked as though they would have a long job trying to gain the necessary information. Still, he was inclined to agree with Randall; there was something suspicious about Lawrence, something indefinably wrong. Perhaps he was only a petty criminal or a black marketeer, but he was just a little bit too cool, too unconcerned. A genuinely innocent man would have been more anxious, more questioning, Tyler felt.

He nodded to Randall and they left the cell. Outside, Tyler said, "I want him thoroughly investigated. I want a forgery expert to scrutinise his papers and I want his story checked out, especially his previous address. Try to find out who the girl in the photo is as well.

"I want to find out if Lawrence is an assassin or some piddling little crook who's too terrified to say anything. Got it?"

"Yes, sir. Shouldn't take too long."

Paul was a few minutes early with the phone call; he was anxious to learn what 'Jaguar' had said to Anton, who should have reported in by now. He went through the coded introductions before asking:

"Has Lawrence been in touch?"

"No, he hasn't. He missed his usual time."

Paul was more annoyed than worried at this; there might well be a good reason but Jaguar's message had sounded as though it had been urgent. "When's his next time?"

"Three hours from now."

"Right, I'll phone back then."

"Mr Keen, I've had a message from Mr Adams."

Paul's attention, which had been wandering, was suddenly focussed. 'Adams' was Canaris' codename for this operation. "And?"

"It reads 'The objective is most regal.' That's all."

For a moment, Paul was nonplussed; the message did not correspond to any of the prearranged cyphers. Then it hit him. Canaris was almost using plain language. He was identifying 'Faust'.

The King of England. King George the Sixth.

"Oh, bloody hell," he muttered.

"Come on, Vogel. We know you're lying. 22, Cedar Road was destroyed by a bomb—very convenient for you—but none of the neighbours remember seeing you. You said you'd been living there for six months. Are you trying to tell us that none of them ever saw you?" Tyler stared impatiently at Anton.

"I travel around a lot. I wasn't there very often."

"Where do you get your brushes from?" This from Randall.

"I've told you. Mitchell and Aldridge in Walthamstow."

"They only have a record of one sale to you, Vogel." Tyler again.

"I'm not Vogel."

"Two weeks ago. Nothing before that. Or since. Yet you haven't sold any since then, have you? Not a very successful salesman, are you?"

"Business is bad. Anyway, it's not a crime to be a poor salesman, is it, for God's sake?"

Tyler ignored this. "Where did you get your supplies from, before that?"

"I've told you. Mitchell and Aldridge."

"They have no records of you before two weeks ago."

"Look, it's not my fault if their system's useless, now, is it? You tell them to look again."

"We have, Vogel. They've never heard of you. That's hardly surprising, is it? There's no such person as Antony Lawrence. You don't exist. I've even checked with Somerset House for your non-existent birth certificate. Is their system useless as well? Your papers are forgeries. Good ones, I'll admit, but forgeries all the same. Who are you? I'll tell you.

"You are a German agent, are you not?"

Anton shook his head slowly, as if in despair; he was not entirely acting. There was no way now that he could talk his way out of this situation; all he could hope for now was to hold out long enough for Paul to escape. He had to lay another false trail.

"Look, I'm not a German spy, if that's what you're getting at," he said slowly. "I'll come clean. I'm not a brush salesman. I'm in the black market. The brushes are just for cover."

Tyler glared at him. "Your real name?"

"David Skinner."

"Previous address?"

"Cedar Road, like I said. I only ever came and went at night. The Greens knew what I was up to and they didn't want the neighbours to cotton on."

Tyler looked at Anton for a long moment. It could be true. It would explain a lot but it would take time to check. He had to hand it to Lawrence; either he was telling the truth or he was responding to the interrogation in the classically effective manner; inventing plausible stories that had to be checked, buying time for his colleagues. Tyler hoped that, if he were ever in Lawrence's position, he would do the same.

"What do you sell on the black market, Skinner?"

"Anything I can get hold of. Food, stockings, cigarettes, anything."

"Where do you get your supplies?"

"Ah, come on. You can't expect me to tell you that."

"But I do, Skinner. Every detail." He gestured to Randall. "Take Mr Skinner, give him some paper and a pen, and tell him to write out a complete list of his sources of supply. Go with him, Skinner."

Anton did not look at Tyler as he went past. If only one man were escorting him, there was a chance he could escape, make a run for it. But Tyler didn't strike him as the sort who'd make such a stupid mistake . . .

When Anton was about a yard beyond him, Tyler called, sharply, "Skinner!"

Anton turned quickly, the thought already forming in his mind that Tyler's ruse was patently obvious, hoping he would not react to the name . . .

Tyler's fist smashed into his jaw, sending Anton reeling backwards. He sprawled in the corner, blood already pouring from his mouth.

Tyler was oblivious to Randall's shocked expression. He had done it; now he knew he was dealing with no black marketeer. In the second or so between Anton turning round and the blow landing, Tyler had seen the other man beginning to react, to parry the blow, then, realising his mistake, he had relaxed, allowing the punch to land. The initial response, however, had been what Tyler had been looking for, the response of a man trained in unarmed combat; highly trained at that—his reaction had been almost instantaneous.

He grabbed Anton by the shirt front and dragged him back to the chair. "Right, Vogel. Maybe you've been told in RSHA headquarters that we British are too gentlemanly to torture their prisoners but don't you believe it. We've learned that the only way to survive is to fight dirty so if you don't start telling the truth, we'll really start hurting you. Understand?"

Anton, who until now had been holding his hand to his mouth, now held it in front of his face, staring at it. "I'm bleeding!" he protested. "What did you hit me for?" His voice was shocked, outraged.

"Vogel—"

"I've told you. It's Skinner. David Skinner."

Tyler sighed to himself. It was going to be a long, hard night.

Harcourt paused briefly at the door, hesitating, wondering whether to take the irrevocable step; in reality, of course, he had taken it two years before, when he had been recruited by the Abwehr. He touched his jacket pocket, feeling the reassuring bulk of the revolver. He felt an impulse to turn and wave to the man he knew must be following him but he restrained himself. The man must not realise he had been spotted or he might decide to arrest Harcourt there and then, before he had carried out this last act.

He had always accepted the possibility of being "blown" by M15 and he had long ago decided what he would do if he had any warning. He had seen Anton being arrested, just after speaking to him and had known he had only hours left. The only reason he had not yet been arrested himself was probably that they were waiting to see who else he contacted but they would not wait long. All he needed was a few more hours, however . . .

He had gone back to the office for the afternoon, forcing himself to act normally. He dictated memos in his usual calm, precise way, joking as always with his secretary, even being polite to that damned fool, Morris, when he appeared in the office. Not that it would make any difference by then but Harcourt wanted the office staff to say, when questioned, that Mr Harcourt seemed his usual self.

He left his desk tidy, said goodnight to his secretary and left at exactly five o'clock. He walked home, savouring the summer sunshine. He prepared a light snack but found himself unable to eat anything. He took out the old Army Issue revolver that had belonged to his father and cleaned it carefully, loading it with six rounds that his father had kept as a memento of his Army days. He slipped the gun into his pocket and left his flat. He debated whether to leave the door unlocked but, in the end, he locked it, more out of a sense of propriety than anything else. He then walked round to the mews flat off Knightsbridge, where he now stood, hesitating.

He reached into his pocket and took out his key-ring,

selecting a key he had not used in months. He inserted it into the lock and turned it. He opened the door and passed noiselessly into the flat that he used to live in.

That had been before Gloria had finally blighted his career. He had put up with her infidelities for years but then she had gone too far. An affaire with a Permanent Under-Secretary had ended with the PUS's wife suing for divorce; Gloria Harcourt had been named as co-respondent. The scandal had wrecked the PUS's career but he had influential friends; they had ensured that Harcourt's future would be ruined as well. Embittered, he had left Gloria and had walked straight into the arms of the Abwehr. They had paid him well . . . but now it was over.

Silently, he closed the door behind him and stood for a moment, listening. After a few moments, he heard a murmur of voices from upstairs. He smiled to himself and then bent down to remove his shoes. He climbed the stairs, soundless in his stockinged feet and moved across the landing.

The bedroom door was open and he could hear the unmistakeable sounds of sex from within. Typical, thought Harcourt, but appropriate. He took out the gun, cocked it and pushed the door wide open, striding swiftly into the room.

She was beneath the man, her legs coiled around his waist, gasping as he thrust rapidly at her. The man seemed to become aware of the intruder and looked around over his shoulder, his eyes widening in terror as he saw the gun. He opened his mouth, whether to say something, or to cry out, Harcourt never knew, because he shot him, there and then, the bullet taking most of the back of the man's head away.

Gloria, pinned down beneath the corpse, stared wide-eyed at Harcourt. She tried to scream but no sound came. Desperately, she tried to push the body away from her, to escape its loathsome embrace.

"No, Gloria. Don't move," said Harcourt, coldly. "Stay exactly where you are." She froze at his words and lay very still. "Good. When they find you, I want them to know what a common whore you really were." As he spoke, he walked around the bed, until he was level with her shoulders. All the time, her eyes followed him in helpless fascination. He pushed the gun under the man's body until the barrel was pressing against her left breast.

"Goodbye, Gloria."

She screamed, a loud, shrill sound that was cut off abruptly as he squeezed the trigger.

Harcourt looked down at the two bodies, still intertwined in their last embrace and at the growing strain of red on the sheets. He heard a frantic knocking at the front door. His shadower had evidently heard the shots but he was too late. Far, far too late.

He raised the gun to his temple, pressing the warm barrel firmly to his flesh. He felt nothing, no real satisfaction at what he had done but that was irrelevant now. There was only a wistful regret at what might have been if he hadn't met Gloria—but he would never know.

His finger tightened on the trigger. There was a blinding flash of whirling, corruscating light and then there was nothing.

He was completely unaware that his body fell forward, across his dead wife and her lover.

Lockhart returned home at just after six and saw the note lying on the doormat. He unfolded it with trembling hands and read the typewritten message. He was to go to Regent's Park and wait on York Bridge at eight o'clock, where arrangements would be made for the delivery of the camera and the collection of the photographs and negatives. Under no circumstances was he to take the camera itself along; he was to leave it in his flat. There was, of course, no signature.

He looked at the clock. He had better hurry. Quickly, he looked around for a hiding place for the camera and eventually left it under the bed. He took a light raincoat from the peg and left, locking the door carefully behind him.

Vogel watched him leave from across the road. He checked the street for any signs of observation. Finding none, he crossed the road and within a minute was inside Lockhart's flat. It only took him a further thirty seconds to find the camera; within three minutes of entering the block of flats, he was outside again, walking unhurriedly along the street.

"So that's about it," concluded Tyler. "He went round to his ex-wife's, shot her and her boyfriend and then shot himself."

"Why didn't your man prevent it?" asked Fenton, peevishly.

"Cummings only had orders to keep Harcourt under surveillance. The first he knew that anything was happening was when he heard the gunshots and by then it was too late."

"Crime of passion?" mused Fenton, absently.

"That's what the police said but I don't agree. He could have knocked his wife off any time, so why now? Especially just after we've arrested this Lawrence character. He must have seen us arresting Lawrence, realised we were onto him and decided to blow his brains out, taking his wife with him."

"So you're pretty certain that Lawrence is a German agent?"

"I'd say so. Harcourt was his contact."

"Unless it was a crime of passion and has no connection with Lawrence at all. It could just be coincidence."

"I don't like coincidences. Not when the stakes are this high. In any case, Lawrence is certainly not a seedy little black marketeer. He's still hiding something, I'm sure of it."

Fenton nodded agreement. "I tend to agree with you. I think I'd better see this Lawrence. We'll have to persuade him to talk. One way or another."

Tyler looked through the spyhole at Anton, who was lying sprawled on the cell bed and then turned to Fenton.

"He still hasn't talked, sir."

"Really? Thirty-six hours and nothing at all?"

"Not a thing. He's sticking to his black market story."

"What methods have you used?"

"The works. I've even had Chisholm and his thugs work him over." The distaste was evident in Tyler's voice.

"Nothing, apart from various comments on Chisholm's parentage, which I'm inclined to agree with."

"You still feel he is lying?"

"Yes. But there's no evidence. It's intuition as much as anything."

Fenton nodded. He had learned, years ago, never to distrust intuition. In trained men, it often proved invaluable. "Very well," he said, with a sigh. "I suppose we'll have to use Groves."

Tyler looked sharply at Fenton. Groves was known in the building as the Nightmare Man. He had been carrying out research into various drugs and their effect on the human brain for several years and had been seconded to M15 on the strength of his claim that he had developed an improved version of sodium pentothal, the "truth drug". He had achieved some successes over the past eighteen months but there had also been several failures; prisoners who had been left as little more than vegetables, their brains irreparably damaged.

"Poor devil," muttered Tyler, looking through the spyhole again.

"We have no choice. If that really is Vogel in there, then he's part of a murder squad, Tyler. Just remember that. He's here to kill the King."

Tyler nodded wearily. "I suppose you're right."

"Get him sent up to Groves. I'll tell him to go ahead."

Anton was only half aware of being hauled out of his cell by two men he had never seen before. He had no memory of being taken up three flights of stairs into a brightly-lit surgery; he only recovered any sort of awareness of reality when he was being strapped down onto a leather couch.

Tyler winced when he saw Anton. The prisoner's face was swollen and puffy with bruises and he had lost at least two of his teeth. One eye was completely closed, the other only half open. Anton looked as though he were at the end of his resources, both physical and mental, but Tyler knew that in some men such appearances could be deceptive. He suspected that Lawrence was one of those men and would still be difficult to break.

Groves, a short, wiry man in his mid forties, administered the injection personally. He waited for several minutes and then pulled back one of Anton's eyelids. He nodded once in satisfaction.

"What is your name?"

"D—David Skinner."

Groves, Fenton and Tyler exchanged looks of surprise and doubt. Was he telling the truth, after all?

"No, it isn't Skinner, is it?" continued Groves smoothly. "It's Vogel, isn't it? Vogel?"

"No—no. Not Vogel. Not Vogel."

Fenton broke in, speaking in fluent German. "What is it, then?"

"Pardon?"

Fenton repeated his question, still in German.

Anton shook his head. "I—I don't understand."

Once again, Fenton and Tyler exchanged glances; were they mistaken, after all?

"What is your name?" asked Groves, patiently.

"Not Vogel."

"Yes, we know that, but what is it?"

"Not—not Vogel. Lawren—Law—S-Skinner!"

"Lawren?" muttered Tyler to himself and then said, "Is it Lawrence?"

"No—yes. Lorenz—Lawrence."

"That's the first name he gave," muttered Tyler to Feton.

"Yes," replied the other man thoughtfully, "but he said 'Lorenz' first." He raised his voice to address the prisoner. "Lorenz, what is your first name? Your Christian name?"

"Anton—Antony Lawrence."

"Anton Lorenz?" called Groves.

"Yes. No. Antony Lawrence. Not Vogel."

Fenton was intrigued by Anton's insistence that he was not Vogel. "Who is Vogel?"

"Vogel's SS. But I'm not him. I'm not he . . . isn't that correct form? . . . I'm not he . . . reflexive pronoun . . . something like that . . ."

"He's wandering," said Tyler.

"Yes. We'll have to get a move on," said Fenton. "Lorenz, who else is with you?"

"Nobody . . . just me. Not Vogel."

"Who else is with you?" said Fenton again.

"Nobody. Just me . . . not Vogel."

"Why are you here?'

"Not Vogel . . ."

"Why are you here?"

"After Vogel . . . we're looking . . ."

"You said 'We', didn't you?"

"Just me. No-one else," said Anton, abruptly, regaining control of himself. "Just me . . . only me . . ."

"He's going under," murmured Groves. "We haven't much time."

"Why are you here, Lorenz?" asked Tyler.

"Not Lorenz. Lawrence."

"Answer the question!"

"Ask me a hard one . . . that one's too easy . . . never answer easy questions . . . might be trick ones . . . won't catch me that way . . . ask me a hard one . . ." Anton had finally lapsed into German but was losing consciousness.

"Why are you here, Lorenz? Answer!" barked Fenton in German.

"Zu Befehl, Herr Oberst! . . . we are here . . . I am here to find Vogel."

"Repeat, please!" Fenton's astonishment was evident.

"Didn't you hear me . . . I'm sorry . . . we . . . I came to find Vogel . . . find Vogel . . ."

"What were you going to do when you found him?"

"Find Vogel . . . more difficult than we thought . . . than we thought . . . find Vogel . . . I'm so tired . . . want to sleep . . ."

"Wake up, Lorenz!" shouted Fenton.

Groves bent over the prisoner. "No good. He's unconscious."

Fenton glared at Anton in angry frustration. "When can we question him again?"

"Not for another six hours at least."

"Damn!" Fenton strode out of the surgery.

Groves looked down at Anton. "He put up an extraordinary resistance, I must confess."

"Are you saying your drug didn't work?"

"Only partly, I'm afraid. He couldn't possibly have been telling the truth." He looked doubtfully at Tyler. " . . . could he?"

"Don't ask me," said Tyler, curtly. "You're supposed to be the expert. Anyway, you'd better come with me. Fenton will be wanting to ask you some questions himself and you'd better have the right answers."

CHAPTER 7

Fenton was standing by the window, looking down at the street below when Tyler arrived with Groves. He spoke as soon as the other two entered, without turning round.

"So we have to wait six hours before we can resume the interrogation?"

"I'm afraid so. Any sooner and there would be a real risk of permanent damage," Groves replied.

"I'm not worried about that," said Fenton. "Will he be coherent?"

"I doubt it. A second injection now would increase his disorientation. He is a very strong subject indeed. He resisted us for quite some time and would probably do so again. To gain any worthwhile results, I would have to increase the dosage, which in itself would be hazardous even in six hours time. To do so now would almost certainly result in permanent brain damage—and then you'll never get anything out of him. Ever."

"Tyler?"

"I don't suppose six hours will make that much difference, sir. If anything happens during that time, then there's dam' all we could do about it anyway. In any case, the subject is not due to leave his residence until Friday. We have four days' grace."

"Yes," said Fenton reluctantly. "I suppose you're right. It's just that in a situation as vital as this, any delay takes on serious implications." He turned to Groves. "Right. Your professional opinion. Was he telling the truth?"

"I found his story hard to believe."

"That's not what I'm asking. You claim that this drug is foolproof—"

"Virtually foolproof, Fenton. Not absolutely."

"Don't split hairs. What I am asking is whether it is possible for anyone to tell lies while under the influence of your drug. Or was it, in this case, completely ineffective?"

"I see what you mean." Groves somewhat belatedly realised that this was not just an academic exercise. Fenton wanted him to give a categoric opinion. He chose his next words carefully. "It is possible that he was not lying—as far as he was aware."

"What do you mean by that?" demanded Fenton testily.

Groves steepled his fingers. "He may have invented the story beforehand and convinced himself that it was the truth. A sort of self-hypnosis. So he would then be telling what he thought was the truth."

"Self-hypnosis?" said Tyler. "I didn't know that could be done."

"Indeed it can," replied Groves. "An Indian fakir on a bed of nails can convince himself the pain does not exist and so he feels nothing."

"But this self-hypnosis is not an easy thing to accomplish?" continued Tyler.

"No, it isn't," Groves admitted.

"You saw the state Lorenz was in when he was brought in. Could he have been in any fit condition to have performed this act of self-hypnosis?"

"It does require a good deal of will-power and concentration," conceded Groves. "He certainly did not look in any fit state to do so but he may have done so previously. Or he may have been hypnotised by someone else some time ago." He sounded doubtful.

"Dr Groves," interrupted Fenton. "Leaving aside the question as to how plausible Lorenz's story might be, was he or was he not telling the truth?"

Groves hesitated and then said slowly, "To be absolutely frank, I do not know. He may have been under some sort of post-hypnotic suggestion . . . Or the drug might not have had the desired effect . . . I honestly do not know."

"If he is under hypnosis, is there any way of breaking through it?"

"Further treatments with the drug might do it or further hypnotic treatments, perhaps."

"In other words, you can guarantee nothing," said Tyler, succinctly. "And we're back to square one. Who is he, and what is he doing here?"

"You asked me for my professional opinion and I gave it," replied Groves, stiffly.

"Very well," said Fenton. "Please continue with your treatment. It's all we can do at the moment."

Groves left without further comment, closing the door firmly behind him.

"Damned idiot," commented Fenton. "So convinced his precious drug is infallible. Why couldn't he just admit Lorenz was lying instead of giving us all this claptrap about self-hypnosis?"

"Well, he'd hardly admit that it didn't work, would he?" said Tyler mildly.

"No, I suppose not. But you have to admit, Tyler, that it's difficult to believe that Lorenz is not Vogel. I mean, it's a flimsy story, saying he's here to find Vogel. Find him for what? It just doesn't make sense."

"That's precisely why I'm wondering about it. I mean, Lorenz originally had a very plausible story about being a black marketeer. He acted the part beautifully and it was the sort of story that would be very difficult to check. Very convincing, very professional. Then all of a sudden, he comes up with a story that is fragile, to say the least. If he had really wanted to lead us up the garden path he would have stuck to the black marketeer story. It doesn't add up."

Fenton shook his head in disbelief. "Look, Tyler, Lorenz has not produced one single shred of concrete evidence to support his story. He has revealed nothing of any value—he hasn't even told us what Vogel is up to. All he did was to repeat various answers over and over again until he passed out. He is spinning us an elaborate yarn to confuse us and he has succeeded—the mere fact that we are wasting time discussing it now shows how effective it has been. We must get a lot more information—real information—out of him during the next interrogation."

Tyler nodded. "I think we ought to concentrate on what Vogel's doing. He seems willing to talk about that but not about what he himself is doing here. Get him to talk and see what else he gives away."

Fenton nodded. "You could well be right, Tyler."

Groves withdrew the syringe from Anton's arm and straightened up. He counted off sixty seconds on his watch and then nodded to Fenton and Tyler.

"What is your name?" asked Fenton.

"Antony Lawrence."

"Anton Lorenz?"

"Yes . . . No. Lawrence."

"Not Vogel?"

"No . . . not Vogel."

"No, Anton, we know you're not Vogel. We know you want to find Vogel."

"Yes . . . Find Vogel."

"What will you do when you find him?"

"Stop him."

"Stop him? Stop him from doing what?"

"Stop him killing . . . Faust."

Fenton and Tyler exchanged glances. Tyler could see his own uncertainty mirrored in Fenton's eyes. Just what was going on here?

"Who is Faust?"

"Don't know."

"Who is Faust?"

"Told you . . . don't know. Must be somebody important. Trying to find out who he is . . . Paul thinks it's Churchill . . ."

Fenton pounced eagerly. "Paul?"

"Nobody . . . just me . . . not Vogel."

"Who is Paul? Is he with you?"

"Not Vogel . . . not Vogel."

Fenton gave an exasperated sigh; Tyler took over the questioning. "Vogel is going to kill Faust?"

"Yes . . . have to stop him."

"How is he going to do it?"

"Roeder. Dieter Roeder . . . trained marksman . . . uses a rifle . . ."

"So there's Vogel and Roeder. Anyone else?"

"No . . . just the two of them."

"And you and Paul have to stop them?" This was from Fenton.

"Yes . . . No . . . just me . . . nobody else."

"Why do you have to stop Vogel?" asked Tyler.

"Orders."

"Who from? Paul?"

"No . . . not Paul . . . Don't know any Paul . . ."

"Then who gives the orders?"

"Canaris."

Once again, Fenton and Tyler exchanged looks. Tyler leaned forward. "But Canaris is in Germany. How do you get instructions from him? Through Harcourt?"

"Who? Don't know him . . ."

"The man in the park."

"Don't know him . . . just passing the time of day . . . going to see Diana."

"Is he your link with Canaris?"

"Link? . . . Not link . . ." Anton muttered something that sounded like "links", but Tyler couldn't be certain.

"How do you contact Canaris?"

"Never see him . . . only a voice . . ."

"Is it by telephone?"

"Yes . . . No."

"You can't talk to Canaris by telephone. Who do you talk to? Who is your link?"

"Not link . . . Links . . ."

"There is more than one link?" snapped Fenton.

"No . . . only one . . . Links . . ."

It was like a flash of light in Tyler's mind; six months before, M15 had rounded up an Abwehr espionage network in Scotland less than seventy-two hours after they had been landed on the Aberdeenshire coast. They had all been assigned codenames of big cats: Tiger, Leopard, Puma and so on. He took a long shot.

"You mean 'Lynx', don't you? L-Y-N-X?"

"Yes . . . No."

"You talk to Lynx on the telephone?"

"Yes . . . cut out system . . ."

"And does Paul telephone Lynx as well?"

"Yes . . . No. Don't know any Paul."

"What is the number? How do we contact Lynx?"

"No number . . . mustn't tell you . . ."

"Why not? We want to help you find Vogel. We want him too. But we must know how to contact Lynx."

Anton shook his head, desperately. "No . . . no number . . . don't know where they are . . . use telephones . . ."

"Who else telephones Lynx?"

"Me . . . Jaguar . . . and . . . nobody else . . . Not Vogel . . ."

"You haven't got much longer," said Groves quietly. "He's going under."

Tyler ignored him. "Is 'Jaguar' Harcourt? The man in the park?"

"Yes . . . no-one else . . ."

"Paul uses the number as well, doesn't he?"

"He . . . knows the number . . . will be waiting for my report . . . no good to you . . . he'll know . . . you've got me . . . He'll . . . run for it . . ."

"Then you aren't putting him in any danger, are you?"

"No . . . mustn't tell you . . . No!"

"But you must, Anton. We can help him find Vogel, but we must know who he is. Just tell us where we can find him."

"Don't know . . . where he is . . . Only . . . use the phone . . ."

"What is his name? Just tell us his name."

"No . . . false name anyway . . . no good to you . . ."

"Then tell us."

"Paul . . . Paul . . . No! . . . Don't know where he is . . . only contact through Lynx . . . safer . . . safer . . . Not Paul . . . not Vogel . . . wrong name . . . mustn't find Paul . . . he'll . . . get away now . . . find Vogel . . ." Gradually, Anton's voice trailed away into silence.

Tyler looked at his watch; it was nearly three in the morning. When had he last slept? It was becoming difficult to remember. Anton Lorenz, if that was his name, had been under virtually constant interrogation for almost seventy-two hours now and Tyler had been present at every session. But he had to get some sleep sometime . . .

Fenton threw the transcript of the latest interrogation onto the desk with an irritated slap. "So what are we to make of all that, Tyler?"

"Well, it hangs together, sir. We've got to admit that. Everything he's told us ties in with that Abwehr message, even down to the names and their objective. The only thing he hasn't told us is who Faust is, but we know that anyway. We haven't been able to catch him out in one single lie or inconsistency. I'm inclined to believe him."

"What, that he and this Paul are here to protect the King from Vogel?"

"Why not? We know that there are two separate groups, don't we? Vogel and Roeder were the ones who killed Lewis, while Lorenz and Paul came ashore in Suffolk. That makes sense, doesn't it?"

"Which meant that Paul and Lorenz killed Gilmore."

Tyler shrugged awkwardly. "What would you have done in their position?"

Fenton nodded in acknowledgement. "Point taken. Go on."

"We know that there is a faction in Germany that wants to get rid of Hitler and negotiate with us. If they got wind of an assassination attempt of His Majesty, they'd try to prevent it, wouldn't they?"

"They already have. They warned us about Vogel's group."

"Yes, but supposing they also sent in an undercover group to prevent Vogel getting anywhere near the King?"

"If that is the case, then why didn't they tell us about them when they sent us the warning?"

"I can't answer that one," Tyler conceded.

Fenton stood up suddenly and began to pace to and fro behind the desk. "It could all be an elaborate deception, Tyler. You yourself said that Vogel's group could be a decoy to distract us from the real killers—the Suffolk group. Lorenz could have been planted on us to feed us this story. He might even have believed that what he is telling us is the truth; he may have been deliberately sacrificed to mislead us. I wouldn't put that past the SS at all."

"But what about the message from the Abwehr? Are you discounting that?"

"Can we prove it was not the SS who sent it? This whole situation could have been engineered by them."

"You have no evidence to support that, sir."

"And you have none to say that they're not behind it all, do you?" He glared at Tyler for several seconds and then nodded slowly. "I'm sorry Tyler. I have no right to snap at you. Look, I am not saying that I disbelieve Lorenz but we simply cannot afford to take chances. It's the King's life we're talking about, after all. This could be an elaborate SS plot, or Lorenz could be Vogel, or there is no second group at all—we just do not know, Tyler. Our only safe course is to find and arrest every German agent in this country, whatever their motives might be. We have to find Vogel, Roeder and this Paul, whoever he is."

"True, " said Tyler heavily; Fenton had the right of it, of course.

"We have three days left before His Majesty resumes his official engagements," said Fenton. "I shall have to call a meeting with Newton and Weldon, amongst others, and let them know of this latest development. I'd like to be able to give them some encouraging news, of course."

"Well . . . we know how their communications system works."

"What, this 'Lynx'? A voice on a telephone line? It could be another piece of pure invention."

"It's the only lead we have, sir. And it's a logical security system, nearly foolproof. Nobody can betray anybody else, no matter how severe the interrogation. All they can do is to give the telephone number—we could get Lynx that way, but not Paul. Not unless we infiltrate the system."

"And how do you suggest we do that?"

"Keep working on Lorenz. Find out the number and any passwords they use. Lorenz doesn't seem able to keep a lie going for very long under the drug—what he's been doing is to evade questions, but we get there in the end. Get the number and the codewords, then send a message through the system to Paul."

"Set a trap for him, you mean?"

"Exactly, sir."

"Keen here," said Paul as soon as they had gone through the code introductions. "Any messages?"

"One from 'Jaguar'. He wants to meet you at the usual place and time. He said that he had the information you wanted."

"I see. Any news from Lawrence?"

"No. Nothing."

"Did 'Jaguar' say anything about his meeting with Lawrence?"

"No."

"Are you certain it was 'Jaguar'?"

There was a delay of several seconds before the voice replied, "It sounded like him. But it was a very poor line, so

112

I can't be certain. He knew all the correct code introductions."

"I see. Anything else?"

"No."

After he had replaced the telephone and left the phone-box, Paul considered the implications as he walked along the street. He didn't like it at all. It had now been forty-eight hours since Anton had last reported in; it was difficult to avoid the conclusion that 'Jaguar' had been "blown" and that Anton had been arrested when he had turned up for the rendezvous. If this was the case, there had been plenty of time for M15 to break him. He could not reveal the contact's location but he might have given enough away for the British to have faked Jaguar's message—or to have persuaded Harcourt to send it himself. It could be a trap; it was exactly what Paul would do in their position.

On the other hand, it was possible that Anton had been picked up elsewhere; a routine documents check, for example. He might even have been killed while resisting arrest; Paul knew that Anton would try to escape if it was humanly possible. 'Jaguar' might still be in the clear and might well have the documents they needed. If this was the case then Paul had to make the rendezvous; even if the British did not suspect 'Jaguar' yet, it was only a matter of time if Anton was under interrogation. This could be the last chance Paul would have of gaining the information he needed to stop Vogel.

He signed, resignedly; he was going to have to take the risk; the alternative was to abort the mission altogether. Paul would have to make the rendezvous, even though he could be walking into a trap . . .

Tyler and Randall put down the headphones and looked thoughtfully at each other. "So he passed the message on," said Randall.

Tyler nodded. "But 'Paul' sounded suspicious, didn't he?"

"He was certainly worried about not hearing from Lorenz, yes. Do you think he might not turn up for the rendezvous?"

"I certainly wouldn't if I were in his shoes. It all depends how badly he wants information from Harcourt, doesn't it?"

Randall nodded glumly. Both he and Tyler knew that they were playing a long shot. Anton had only revealed the telephone number and passwords six hours before. They had soon traced Lynx's address from his telephone number and had fed him the message purporting to come from Harcourt. It had then been a simple matter to put a tap on his telephone so that they could listen to his conversation with Paul. All that remained was to see if Paul took the bait; if he didn't, they would have lost him altogether. They could only hope for the best . . .

Which still left the problem of what to do about Lynx. Tyler picked up the telephone and dialled a number. It rang twice before it was answered.

"Tyler here. Pick up the subject."

The man known as 'Lynx' felt a sudden stab of premonition as he heard the knock at the door. He had been talking to Paul less than five minutes before; Paul had been worried about Anton's disappearance and now there was someone knocking at his door. Lynx did not believe in coincidences; before answering the door, he took a revolver from a drawer and put it into his jacket pocket.

There were two men standing on the landing outside; Lynx's heart sank as he saw them.

He was blown.

"Mr Ronald Lewinton?"

"Er—yes?"

"I'm Detective Sergeant—"

He got no further. Lynx pulled out his gun and shot the policeman in the chest at point blank range. He traversed the barrel, aiming at the second man but the other policeman reacted instantly, his right arm chopping down on Lynx's wrist, knocking the gun to one side. Lynx barely had time to realise that the other man was trained in unarmed combat before the fist exploded into his stomach like a piston.

He doubled up, gasping, appalled at the power behind the

blow and then the gun was wrenched from his grasp as he was hurled back against the door frame. He allowed himself to collapse as though stunned but his hand dived inside his jacket as he pitched forward. He hit the floor and rolled over; as he did so, his hand moved up to his mouth in a convulsive movement. He bit into the cyanide capsule . . .

The Special Branch man cursed as Lynx began to writhe in agony on the floor. He rammed his fingers down Lynx's throat in an attempt to make him regurgitate the pill, but it was far too late; Lynx's face was already turning blue as the poison took effect.

It took less than twenty seconds for Lynx to die.

"Not the most satisfactory report I have read, Tyler," said Fenton acidly. "First Harcourt and now this Lynx. Both dead. What the devil went wrong?"

"He tried to make a run for it, sir," Tyler replied. "He killed McGregor and tried to shoot Haines; it was all over in a matter of seconds. There wasn't much else Haines could have done. He'd managed to disarm Lynx, after all; he wasn't to know he had a cyanide pill ready to take."

"No, I suppose not," Fenton agreed reluctantly. "But it leaves us with only a tenuous lead to this man Paul. Lorenz can't or won't tell us where he is so we now have no direct links to this man at all."

"Lynx might not have been able to help us much anyway, sir," Tyler observed. "He probably never phoned Paul; he was only on the receiving end of calls. But he might have had an emergency number where he could have contacted Paul."

"Now we'll never know that," snapped Fenton. "All we have is this rendezvous tomorrow. If he turns up." He looked out of the window. "For all our sakes, Tyler, he'd better be there."

Maureen was in the bath when the phone rang. She was tempted to ignore it but then she climbed reluctantly out of the steaming water and wrapped a towel around herself.

"Hello?"

"Hello, Maureen. It's Kenneth Vernon," said Vogel's voice.

"Oh, hello, Mr. Vernon. I'm afraid you've got me out of the bath."

"In that case, I wish I were there. However . . . would you do me a favour, Maureen?"

"Certainly. If I can."

"Would you find out the times of trains to Rochester in the mornings?"

"Any particular morning?"

"No, just the regular services."

"Be glad to."

"Thanks. I'll drop by in a day or so. 'Bye."

"Cheerio."

The line went dead. Maureen stared at the receiver for a few moments and then shrugged. She assumed he had a good reason for not finding out the times himself but she resented being made to run errands. Typical of the man, she thought . . .

But she would be seeing him again; the prospect both dismayed and excited her.

"Oh, Paul . . ." she gasped and then climaxed, holding him tightly as she heard his cry of pleasure. They stared into each other's eyes and then kissed, gently. They lay still for a long time, saying nothing. Eventually, Carolyn whispered:

"What happened, Paul? That was wonderful."

"I know, Carolyn."

"It was better than it's ever been for me. It was—I don't know—special." She smiled at him. "You know—this could be happening quite a lot while Aunt Mary's ill. Mum and Dad might be spending quite a few nights over at her house."

He kissed her gently. "Then we'll really be able to get to know each other, won't we?"

She giggled. "I think we know each other pretty . . . intimately as it is, don't you?"

"You could say that," he chuckled.

She snuggled up close to him and closed her eyes. "Paul?" she murmured.

"Yes?"

"Have you ever been in love?" Her voice was drowsy.

"Yes," he said quietly. "It was a long time ago, though."

"Did you—did you sleep with her?"

"Yes."

"Was it as good with me as it was with her?"

She might be half asleep, thought Paul, but she knows what she's doing . . . He gave her the answer she wanted. "Yes it was, Carolyn." And he was not altogether lying, he realised
. . .

"I'm glad, Paul. I'm glad you felt the same . . . but then . . . you are special . . . to me . . ." She was obviously drifting off to sleep; Paul said nothing. He waited until her breathing had settled down into a steady rhythm and then carefully removed his arm from under her neck. He lay on his back, staring up at the ceiling.

It had been a mistake. He had known it was even before they had come to bed; but how could he have explained his reluctance to take advantage of her parents being away for the night? How to refuse her without hurting her, without appearing to reduce her to the level of a one-night stand?

Paul grimaced in self-disgust. If he were perfectly honest about it, he had wanted to go to bed just as much as she had; why deny it? But there was no doubt that it had complicated the issue. He was becoming involved with Carolyn Marriott; he had not lied when he had told her that their love-making had been special. Knowing that she felt the same way did not exactly help, either . . .

He looked at her face in the darkness. It would be so easy, he realised, just to forget his mission and stay with Carolyn. Especially as the search of Vogel was getting nowhere . . . The prospect of settling down with Carolyn was undeniably appealing.

What was he thinking of? What could he do? If he stayed in London, it would only be a matter of time before the money he had brought with him ran out; how would he explain to her that he was not the clerk she thought he was?

Then call off the operation, go back to Germany, leave her a message saying that he would meet her again when the war was over? His mouth twisted sardonically. How would she feel about him when she discovered his true identity and realised that he had lied to her?

He signed. There had to be a way . . . had to be . . .

Sleep took him completely unawares; and then came the dream . . .

It was an October night, quite mild for the time of year. Paul checked his watch as he turned the corner; it was nearly eight o'clock. There was a black Mercedes with SS number plates parked outside the block of flats where Ilse lived; he quickened his pace, filled by a dread premonition, reaching the front steps just as two Gestapo agents came out. Between them was Ilse, pale faced, terrified. She saw Paul and twisted violently in their grip, trying to break free.

"Paul! For God's sake, help me!"

"What is happening?" Paul demanded, producing his pass. The taller of the two agents glanced at it indifferently; Gestapo men were not easily impressed by anybody.

"Orders, sir."

A third man, dressed in SS uniform, appeared in the doorway. Paul turned to him.

"May I enquire what is happening, Sturmbannfuehrer?" The words were polite but Paul's tone was icy.

The officer glanced at his pass. "Koenig, eh? Your name is not unknown, even at Prinzalbrechtstrasse. You know this woman?"

"Yes."

"She is being taken for questioning."

"On what grounds?"

"State security," the Sturmbannfuehrer said flatly.

Paul quickly assessed the other man. A protestation of Ilse's innocence would have no effect at all. "I see," he said, his face and voice expressionless. "Your name, please?"

For the first time, the other man looked uncertain. "Sturmbannfuehrer Brunner."

"Very well, Sturmbannfuehrer Brunner, I shall report this matter as well as your lack of co-operation to the appropriate authorities. Reichsfuehrer Himmler will be interested, no doubt." He was bluffing, in that he was only distantly acquainted with Himmler, but he hoped it would have some effect.

He saw Brunner's momentary hesitation before he came to a decision. "You may do so if you see fit. I have my instructions. Please stand aside." He pushed brusquely past Paul.

Paul turned to assess the situation. He was too late. Ilse was already in the car between the two Gestapo men in the back seat—physical action was out of the question now. Brunner climbed into the front passenger seat, while Paul watched helplessly. If only he had acted as soon as they had brought her out! He could have dealt with the two Gestapo men and—then what? A run for it, when Brunner and the other two were virtually certain to be armed? Drag the driver out, take over the car and drive off? Too long—Brunner would have been on the scene by then, gun in hand. And even if by some miracle they succeeded in escaping, where would they go?

Despite this, it took all of his self-control to stand and watch as the car drove away. He could see Ilse's face through the rear window as she looked back at him. And there was nothing he could do to save her . . .

"Ilse! Ilse!"

"Paul! Wake up, Paul!"

"Eh?" His eyes flickered open. Where was he? He looked at the girl beside him; it was Carolyn. This was London, not Berlin . . .

"Sorry," he mumbled. "Bad dream."

"It's all right," she murmured. There was a silence that lasted for several seconds and when she spoke, Paul knew that she had been plucking up courage to ask the question. "Paul?"

"Yes?"

"Who . . . who is Ilse?"

Paul's features showed no reaction but, inside, he was appalled. What the devil was he thinking of, making such an elementary breach of security? Then came a deeper fear: had he spoken in German in his sleep? "Ilse?" he asked, stalling for time.

"You shouted it out in your sleep."

"Did I? Sorry about that. Did I say anything else?"

"No. You just repeated 'Ilse' over and over again." There was more than a hint of jealous suspicion in her voice.

Paul relaxed, but only slightly. The situation was still potentially dangerous. He had to offer some explanation, not just to placate her but also to allay any suspicions she might have if she were to think about it later on. "She was a girl I knew before the war. She was working in the German Embassy over here. We became—very close—but then she had to go back to Germany. We lost touch with each other but I heard what happened to her. She—she's dead now."

"Oh God, Paul. I'm so sorry. I shouldn't have poked my nose in."

Paul hardly heard her; his thoughts were far away, reliving Ilse's arrest. It had been the last time he had ever seen her; she had been involved in the Anti-Hitler Conspiracy and had been tortured unmercifully before she had died. Paul had joined the Conspiracy himself only weeks after her death . . . "It's all right, Carolyn. You weren't to know."

"Was she . . . was she the girl you were in love with?"

"Yes."

She pressed herself against him as if offering him comfort. "How did she die, Paul?" she whispered.

It had all been a pipedream, Paul realised. The idea of abandoning the operation and settling down with Carolyn had been no more than that. The only reason he had entertained it at all was that he knew he was probably going to be walking into a trap tomorrow when he went to meet 'Jaguar'. But the dream had reminded him of his purpose. He could not give up the mission; to do so would be to betray Ilse.

"She was killed by a man named Vogel," he said, softly.

CHAPTER 8

Paul walked slowly through the park on his way to the rendezvous with 'Jaguar'. He was deep in thought but not about his mission. Try as he might, he could not keep Carolyn out of his mind. He was aware of an overwhelming sense of loss; he knew that what he felt for her could have grown into something deep and lasting if things had been different . . . But they were not and he had a job to do.

Paul may have been preoccupied, but as he approached the rendezvous at the Serpentine Bridge, his trained reactions began to re-assert themselves. He scrutinised his surroundings carefully.

He paused and began to rummage through his pockets as though searching for something. He took note of the scene. There was no sign of 'Jaguar' but that was not necessarily suspicious—there was a fifteen minute period for the contact and only five had passed.

What concerned Paul was that there were too many people around, too many men who looked fit and healthy, as though they ought to be serving in the armed forces and not idling about in Hyde Park.

His fears had been justified; it was a trap.

Paul finished hunting through his pockets and began to walk on; to turn back would attract attention.

It was obvious to Paul that Anton or 'Jaguar' had cracked and that the British had managed to extract the details of the communication system. The only further question to be answered was whether they had a description of Paul or whether they were merely waiting for someone to show up at the rendezvous. If they had a description, he was finished. If not, he might yet bluff his way out.

He crossed the bridge and began to stroll towards the gate as though he had all the time in the world. He did not dare to look round. He put his hands into his trouser pockets and slouched forward, which made him appear shorter and more thick-set. He also adopted a shuffling gait that made him look rather older.

There were three men standing by the gate but there was nothing else he could do but to keep going. They were about twenty yards away, now. One was looking straight at him but there was no sign of recognition; none of them moved. The one who was watching him was leaning casually against the stone gate post. The second was on the far side of the gate, lighting a cigarette, about five yards from the first, to the left. The third was ten yards along the street, to the right; Paul could see him through the railings.

Ten yards to go.

The nearest man, the one who was watching him, looked behind Paul. No moves were made. There was no sign of alarm or recognition . . .

Paul's hopes began to rise . . .

Tyler looked at his watch for about the fiftieth time; there was no sign of anybody turning up for the rendezvous. It was beginning to look as though the deception had failed; even so, it had been worth a try. It was possible that someone had turned up but had spotted the trap; without a reliable description, they had no way of identifying him. Lorenz had proved to be unbreakable on this count in that each description he had given had been a carbon-copy of Adolf Hitler. If nothing else, Lorenz had proved that Groves' drug was, at best, only partly successful against a determined man.

Tyler began to walk slowly towards the Knightsbridge gate, where Randall was on duty. About twenty yards ahead of him was a slouching figure, hands thrust deep in his pockets; Tyler barely noticed him.

It was all pure chance. Tyler saw Randall at the gate and beckoned him, intending to ask him if he had seen anything out of the ordinary. All Randall saw, however, was Tyler raising his arm. He interpreted this as a signal to stop the man just about to pass through the gate; he missed Tyler's beckoning gesture.

"Excuse me, sir," he said to the slouching man, holding out a detaining arm.

Paul's fist exploded into Randall's solar plexus without any warning. Randall doubled up, clutching his stomach; Paul headed straight for the man with the cigarette, who was staring open-mouthed at Randall.

Paul's left hand shot out, chopping into the man's throat as he went past. The man with the cigarette reeled back into the railings and then fell heavily forward, unconscious.

Tyler watched, aghast, as Paul sprinted down Knightsbridge, directly away from Cummings, the third man. Tyler was awe-struck; their quarry had just incapacitated Randall and Baxter, both trained in unarmed combat; he'd moved like lightning. Cummings was tearing after Paul but he was already thirty yards behind. Tyler began to run, ignoring the pain from his leg.

Paul pounded along, desperately looking for any form of cover; if he could get rid of his tattered raincoat and change the image, he could still get out in one piece.

He dived into a side street, risking a swift backward glance. His nearest pursuer was about thirty yards behind with another about the same distance further back. There were two others but they were well behind; he could afford to ignore them for the moment.

He had to find cover. A running man was too conspicuous; a man obviously being pursued could be stopped in any number of ways—an outstretched foot being the most likely. Paul turned another corner and skidded to a halt, removing his coat. He held it two-handed like a matador with his cape.

Cummings came hurtling around the corner and Paul whipped the coat over the running man's head. Before Cummings could even begin to realise what had happened, Paul hit him with a powerful two-handed blow to the head. As Cummings reeled back, Paul bounded up the front steps of a block of flats and into the lobby.

Once inside, he looked quickly around. There was no-one in sight; for about the next five seconds or so, he would be unobserved. He could see the flight of stairs up to the first floor; it was tempting but far too obvious.

He would have to gamble on the chance that none of his immediate pursuers had seen him close up; only the two at the park gates had seen him from anything closer than twenty yards and neither of them were going to be fit to walk, much less run, for several minutes.

Paul sprawled in the corner, clutching his stomach. His face was contorted in an expression of pain and he was gasping for breath, clearly in distress.

No sooner had he done so when the door flew open and Tyler came in. His eyes swept the lobby and saw Paul huddled in the corner. He crouched over Paul.

"Which way did he go?"

Paul didn't raise his head; he merely pointed at the stairs. "He . . . hit . . . me . . . the bastard . . . hit me!" he gasped.

"We'll get him, don't worry." Tyler stood up and signalled through the open door. Two men came in, panting. "He's gone up the stairs," he told them. "Harrison, you come with me—we'll check each floor and the roof. Peters, you check the fire escape."

Paul watched them go; as soon as they were out of sight, he jumped to his feet and walked briskly out of the building, ignoring the semi-conscious Cummings lying on the pavement.

He was some way down the street before the reaction hit him. That had been close; too close. He had relied completely on the assumption that his pursuers would expect him to keep on running, that he would not stop and allow them to overtake him. Now, he found himself literally shaking—it had been nearly impossible to lie there, waiting, when every impulse had been screaming at him to get up and run.

He forced himself to think clearly. He now knew for certain that Anton and 'Jaguar' were blown, as was the communication system. It was too dangerous to remain in London. More to the point, it was now futile; 'Jaguar' had been their last real hope of gaining any useful information.

There was, quite simply, nothing else left to do.

His shoulders sagged in defeat. The mission was over.

Tyler swore in frustration. Each landing had been deserted, as was the roof. They had lost him, unless he was hiding in one of the flats; somehow he doubted it. Their quarry could have escaped via the rear door or over the roof—why would he risk being trapped in a flat, knowing that they were bound to be searched?

"Right, we'll have to search the flats. I don't suppose it'll do much good—I think he's scarpered but we'll have to give it a go. Peters, you take the top floor, Harrison the first and I'll take the ground. I'll have a word with that bloke in the hall he clobbered—he might be able to give us a description."

The irony of these words was not lost on Tyler when he reached the lobby and found that their quarry's apparent victim was nowhere to be seen.

"You idiot, Tyler!" he shouted, in bitter chagrin. "You were damned well talking to him!"

He sat on the bottom stair, shaking his head in disbelief. Then he began to smile, despite himself. Of all the bloody cheek! You had to hand it to him, Tyler thought, he'd fooled the lot of them. He certainly didn't lack brains or nerve.

His smile faded. Which only makes him all the more dangerous, he thought, grimly.

Vogel entered the block of flats where Lockhart lived, using the front entrance, although he had checked the street for any signs of surveillance; he was mildly interested to see that it had been withdrawn. He had no way of knowing that the surveillance of Lockhart's flat by the Special Branch had been called off twenty-four hours before on Fenton's instructions; he was convinced that Harcourt had been the contact and so watching Lockhart's flat was a manifest waste of time. Vogel was unconcerned whether the flat was under surveillance or not; it would make no difference to his course of action.

Vogel paused briefly on the first floor landing and took his automatic pistol from his jacket pocket. He produced a four-inch perforated cylinder from the other pocket and screwed this onto the gun barrel. He knocked on Lockhart's door, holding the gun in his right hand, cocked, ready to fire.

It was going to be so ridiculously easy, thought Vogel. Lockhart would open the door and Vogel would shoot him in the heart, the silenced gunshot barely audible beyond ten yards or so. The impact of the soft nosed bullet would fling Lockhart backwards into his flat and that would be it . . .

The door began to open. Simultaneously, Vogel heard the street door opening behind and below him. Whoever it was would only see his back as they came into the lobby, but they would still hear the muffled report of the shot and the sound of Lockhart's body hitting the floor . . .

Vogel came to an instant decision. He pocketed the gun, just as Lockhart appeared in the doorway. He was a sitting duck, thought Vogel, but he was only too aware of the footsteps in the lobby.

"Mr Lockhart?" he asked, in the bored tones of an official making a routine enquiry.

"Er—yes."

"My name's Lister. I'm on Mr Parsons' staff at the Ministry. May I come in?"

"Er—yes, certainly." Lockhart stood aside to let Vogel enter.

As he pushed past, Vogel's eyes swept the small bed-sit; Lockhart was alone. He turned to face his victim.

Lockhart closed the door and turned towards his visitor. Vogel's foot slammed into Lockhart's groin, brutally crushing his testicles. Lockhart doubled up in agony, his mouth open in a silent scream.

Vogel stepped behind the other man and grabbed Lockhart's jaw in both hands. He yanked Lockhart's head to one side in a sudden twisting movement. There was an audible crack as Lockhart's neck snapped like a rotten twig and his body went suddenly limp. Vogel released his grip and watched impassively as Lockhart's body sprawled untidily on the floor.

The killer went to the door and listened. He could hear the

footsteps on the second flight of steps, growing fainter. He waited until they began on the third flight and then relaxed.

He looked around the flat again and donned a pair of gloves. He crossed to the chest of drawers beside the bed and opened the bottom drawer, throwing its contents haphazardly across the floor. He did the same to the other drawers. He wanted it to look as though there had been a burglary in which the intruder had been surprised and had killed Lockhart in a fight. It would not hold up for very long, but it would cause a delay, if nothing else.

Vogel asked for the number McConville had given him; it was answered on the second ring.

"Hallo?" It was a woman's voice.

"I'd like to talk to Sean, please."

"Just a minute. I'll get him. Who shall I say is calling?"

"Ken Vernon."

There was a pause and then Vogel heard McConville's voice. "Hallo, Ken. What can I do for you?"

"Thought you might fancy a pint at the local."

"Sounds a good idea, Ken. When?"

"How soon can you get there?"

"Nine o'clock?"

"Nine o'clock it is. See you then, Sean."

McConville reached the pub at nine o'clock exactly; Vogel watched him from a doorway opposite. As soon as McConville had gone inside, Vogel left the doorway and walked rapidly along the street in the direction from which McConville had come. He turned into an alleyway and then stopped, to wait.

True to their procedure for a missed rendezvous, McConville only remained in the pub for fifteen minutes. Vogel watched him as he emerged and walked hurriedly towards him. McConville was about five yards away when Vogel called:

"Sean! In here!"

The Irishman flicked a glance in his direction, nodded imperceptibly and then turned into the alley as though he had been intending to do so all along. "What's up?"

"You're being followed, Sean," said Vogel tersely.

"Holy Mother of God! Who by?"

"I don't know. He's hiding in that doorway opposite the pub at the moment. I was watching the pub myself when you arrived and I saw him tailing you."

McConville nodded and began to turn away from Vogel. Perhaps he caught a glimpse out of the corner of his eye of Vogel reaching inside his jacket, or perhaps it was simply a finely developed sense of survival, but, whatever the reason, he pivoted round to face Vogel as the German brought out a wicked-looking stiletto knife.

"No!" McConville yelled and sprang to one side as Vogel lunged forward with the knife. McConville's right hand chopped down on Vogel's forearm, knocking the knife to one side and then the Irishman's left fist came scything around at Vogel's head. With an almost graceful twist, Vogel dodged away from the blow, but the action threw him off balance; he stumbled two or three steps before he regained his equilibrium.

McConville's hand plunged into his coat pocket and emerged gripping a snub-nosed automatic pistol; he flicked off the safety catch and brought the gun up in a single motion. His finger was already tightening on the trigger as Vogel leaped forward, the knife slashing viciously down at McConville's gun-hand.

McConville screamed as the blade sliced through his wrist, the blood gushing from the severed artery; the gun fell from his suddenly nerveless fingers and clattered to the ground. Vogel drew back his arm to deliver the killing thrust . . .

But McConville wasn't finished yet; he ignored the agony in his right wrist and twisted aside a second time. His left hand snaked down and grabbed Vogel's wrist in a vice-like grip, holding the knife away from him. For perhaps two seconds, the two men stood locked in a frozen tableau and then Vogel's left fist drove into McConville's stomach like an express train.

128

McConville gasped and leaned forward, fighting for breath, but still he clung on to Vogel's wrist.

Vogel jerked back his right arm, pulling McConville after it and slammed his left fist into McConville's jaw, breaking it with the savage force behind the blow. McConville reeled back against the wall and, a second time, Vogel's fist slammed into his solar plexus. Vogel finally tore his wrist free from the Irishman's grasp; McConville was only vaguely aware of Vogel grabbing his hair and lifting his head up. He saw the knife coming at him but he was powerless to move as it was rammed into his chest, just below the ribs. He bellowed in agony as Vogel forced the blade in up to the hilt; it felt as though a white hot poker were being driven through him . . .

Vogel yanked the knife out and stepped back so that none of the blood would spill onto him. McConville stared wildly at Vogel and then looked down at the growing stain of red on his chest. He took two tottering steps towards his killer, whom he could now hardly see; Vogel was disappearing into a deepening red mist in front of his eyes. He felt his legs begin to buckle.

"You . . . bastard, Vogel!" he gasped and then fell heavily forward. His left arm reached out towards Vogel in mute accusation and then his body shuddered convulsively in a last paroxysm of agony.

Vogel leaned against the wall, his chest heaving as he sucked in great gasps of air. That had been close . . . too damned close; but there was no time for such introspection. He carefully wiped the knife blade on McConville's coat and then rolled the body over. To his surprise, he found himself unable to look at McConville's face, knowing what he would see in the lifeless eyes. Must be getting soft, he thought scathingly, as he reached inside the dead man's jacket. He took out the wallet, which he pocketed and then did the same with McConville's gun. Glancing quickly around to see if he had left behind any incriminating evidence, Vogel walked unhurriedly out into the street. With any luck, the police would assume that robbery had been the motive for the attack and that the dead man had put up a fight . . . It would probably be several days before they even managed to identify the body.

He had to admit to himself that he had not really wanted to kill McConville but there had been no alternative. The only way to guarantee that there would be no IRA interference had been McConville's death. The IRA would be furious, but there would soon be no way for them, or M15, to follow his trail; the only remaining person who could implicate or identify Vogel was Maureen and, before the night was over, she would not be able to tell anybody anything.

Just one more, and Vogel would have covered his tracks completely.

Maureen looked at her watch as she heard the knock at the door: Vogel was dead on time—as always. She opened the door.

"Hallo," she said brightly.

His answering smile was surprisingly warm. "Hallo, Maureen. May I come in?"

"Of course." She stood aside to let him pass. "Help yourself to a seat."

"Thank you." He sat down on the sofa; she sat in the armchair facing him. "Did you get those train times?"

"Yes." She had written the times down on a slip of paper but she could remember them easily enough. "They leave Waterloo at ten in the morning and one in the afternoon. It's a two hour journey. Is that what you wanted?"

"Excellent."

She looked at him. "Did you come all this way just for me to give you some train times?"

"No. I've some good news for you. Our operation has been completely successful."

"You mean you got what you wanted from him?"

"Everything. I shall make sure your superiors know how well you carried out your part."

She grimaced. "Don't remind me."

"At least you won't have to do it any more."

"I'm not sorry about that." She looked at him. "So what happens to me, now?"

130

"You go back to McConville and resume your previous existence with the IRA."

"And you?"

"You don't need to know that."

She glared at him. "You know, you're a cold so-and-so. Look, I've had to behave like a complete slut and I don't even get told why."

Vogel stared at her as if making up his mind. Then he nodded. "Very well. It won't do any harm, I suppose. It's an assassination job. Lockhart gave us some information we needed. And you helped us to get it."

"Assassination? Who? Someone important?"

"Very."

"Who? Churchill?"

"No. Even more important."

"More important than Churchill?" Then realisation hit her. "Good God," she whispered. "Not King George?" Vogel nodded, smiling as if at some secret joke. She grinned. "You certainly think big, I'll give you that." She stood up and went into the kitchen. When she returned, she was carrying two glasses and a bottle of whisky. "I think this calls for a little celebration, doesn't it? Care to join me?"

"Yes," said Vogel. "But not in a drink."

She tensed. "What do you mean?"

"I was thinking of a different kind of celebration. In bed."

She stared at him for several seconds and then put down the bottle and glasses. "Why not?" she said smiling. She began to unbutton her blouse, suddenly aware how much she was trembling. She realised just how badly she had always wanted to go to bed with him; and yet she didn't even like him very much . . . She led the way into the bedroom; they stood on opposite sides of the bed and, without a word to each other, they undressed.

He was not gentle with her, but she did not want him to be. Their coupling was frantic and the sound she made at her climax was more like a cry of pain than of pleasure. Yet she was fulfilled, completely so; she had never enjoyed it so much before. We're two of a kind, she thought contentedly as she

lay basking in the afterglow. We both want the same things
. . .

They lay still for several seconds, then he shifted position,
so that he was kneeling astride her hips. She closed her eyes
as his hands ran lightly over her body; she smiled to herself.
Surely he didn't want her again already? If he did, she would
be only too glad to oblige . . . His hands moved upwards to
her throat, caressing her gently . . .

The sudden, suffocating pressure took her totally by
surprise. His hands were pressing down in a vice-like grip,
choking her. Desperately, she tried to wriggle free, but his
weight was pinning her down securely; she could not throw
him off, nor could she bring her knee up into his groin.

Frantically, she tried to prise loose his grip, knowing it
would be in vain. She pummelled at his arms, chest, back,
finally his face, but to no avail; he seemed immovable,
immune to her blows. It was as though he were an automaton,
a killing machine.

Then she looked into his eyes and knew, beyond any
remaining doubt, that there would be no escape. His eyes
were totally without emotion. They always had been, she
thought, only she had never noticed before. They were dead,
the eyes of a killer; and deep down, she realised, she had
always known this. Abruptly, she stopped struggling, her
body accepting the inevitability of death.

One last thought came to her before the final darkness
descended . . .

Why?

Vogel dressed quickly, ignoring the naked body on the bed;
there was still no expression at all in his eyes.

As he dressed, he looked quickly around the flat. It was
unlikely that there would be any incriminating evidence but it
was as well to be sure. He began to search the flat,
methodically, opening the bottom drawers of the dressing
table first. Once again, he began to scatter the contents
around the room. The police's first impressions would be rape
and burglary. They would soon think otherwise once they

realised that her boyfriend had been murdered on the same night, but they might well assume it was a jealous lover.

He pulled back the carpet and checked underneath. Nothing. Nor was there anything in the cistern. No tell-tale rents of stitching in the armchairs; nothing had been stuffed into their innards. Nor was there anything in the mattress, as far as he could tell.

Vogel was just checking behind the wardrobe when a knock at the door interrupted him.

Paul stood on the pavement opposite Maureen's flat, looking up at the lighted window. He was still uncertain as to his reasons for being here; the operation was effectively at an end now. Nobody would think any the worse of him if he abandoned it and went back to Germany. There was an automatic signalling device buried in the dunes near where Gilmore had met his death; all he had to do was to activate it to be picked up by an E-boat within twelve hours of the signal being transmitted. That would be the prudent course; simply cut and run.

But the mission was not quite dead yet; he had not explored every last avenue. He had no evidence that Maureen Riordan was connected with Vogel but it had to be regarded as a possibility. Until he had definitely established that she was innocent, there was still a slender chance that he could locate Vogel. The only way to confirm or deny her link with Vogel was to confront her . . . He shook his head at his own folly; why hadn't he just made a run for it? Did catching Vogel mean that much to him?

He already knew the answer to that; he would not be here otherwise. He crossed the street and went into the lobby. As he mounted the stairs, he debated what strategy to use with her. He had a forged police identification card—nothing like the real thing, but most people didn't know what the genuine article looked like anyway. A direct approach might well bring results. If not, he might have to use less pleasant methods . . .

He knocked briskly at the door, trying to make the knock sound as official as possible. There was no sound from within.

Paul glanced down; there was a chink of light shining under the door. The light was on; someone was in but was not answering the door . . .

Paul took out his silenced automatic, took careful aim and fired. The lock splintered and the door swung open a few inches. He flattened himself against the wall next to the door-hinge and waited.

There was no sound.

Slowly, using his foot, he pushed the door open and then slammed it back on its hinges. He waited for any reaction from inside and then peered cautiously into the flat.

Nothing. There was no-one behind the door, nobody in the living-room. He began to feel a little ridiculous but he never took his eyes from the bedroom and bathroom doors as he moved slowly into the flat, closing the door behind him.

The bedroom door was half-open. Paul cautiously approached it, once again flattening himself against the wall and gently eased the door open.

In one rapid movement, he leaped into the room, dropped immediately into the pistol-shooting crouch and lined up his gun on the two shadowy figures by the bed.

In the split second before Vogel acted, Paul saw that the other man was holding the naked girl in front of him; he had no time to realise that she was already dead before Vogel threw the girl's body straight at him.

Paul could not shoot at what he thought was a living, helpless girl, nor was he given any chance to avoid her. The girl's weight threw him off balance, sending him crashing into the wall; he saw Vogel already coming at him in a flying drop-kick, feet aimed at his head.

Paul twisted to one side; the feet slammed into his left shoulder. He fell heavily; Vogel landed and was on his feet in an instant, aiming a vicious kick at Paul's kidneys. Paul rolled away, taking the blow on his chest, his hands snaking out to grab Vogel's ankle. Paul rose to his knees, lifting and twisting at the ankle. Vogel reeled back but managed to wrench his ankle free of Paul's grip.

Paul dived across the floor after Vogel; there was no time to search for his gun, which had been thrown from his hand by

Vogel's drop-kick. Vogel was too fast, too skilled at unarmed combat.

Vogel saw him coming and brought his legs up into Paul's stomach, straightening them with an explosive gasp, propelling Paul over his head, straight towards the wall.

That should have finished it but Paul twisted round in mid-air, slapping backwards with both hands as he landed to soften the impact. He rose to his feet, just as Vogel came upright.

Both men eyed the other, warily. Both men now knew how expert the other was; Paul had known this anyway, but Vogel was having to come to terms with the fact that this intruder was quite possibly his equal or even his superior at unarmed combat. He looked familiar, somehow . . .

Koenig. Paul Koenig; the name came to him in a flash of revelation. He was faced by one of the most highly trained agents in the Abwehr; what was he doing here?

Deliberately, Vogel ignored the problem; it was an irrelevant and possibly fatal distraction, as was his self-recrimination about not using a gun from the start. He had been too confident in his own ability to handle the situation without it. Now, there was no time to produce the gun; Paul would have him in an instant. Now, he had to get out—kill Paul, if possible, but escape was the main consideration.

Paul swept a jewellery box from the dressing table and hurled it at Vogel's face. Paul leaped in after it as Vogel's hands came up to protect himself.

Paul went for Vogel's groin, left hand slamming viciously upwards but he didn't quite make contact. He heard Vogel's grunt of pain, then Vogel locked his hands together and smashed a two-handed blow down onto Paul's neck. Paul fell heavily forward but rolled away from the following kick. He slapped his palms down onto the floor and came to his feet, facing Vogel.

He was till not quite on balance, however, when Vogel came at him again with a powerful left-handed strike at the neck. Paul blocked it one-handed, simultaneously aiming a straight-fingered blow at Vogel's solar plexus. Vogel moved sufficiently to make the blow miss its target; it was painful but no more than that. However, he doubled up, as if Paul had struck home, knowing what the next move would be—a two-handed blow to the back of the neck.

As Paul's arms were raised to deliver the final blow, Vogel lunged forward and butted Paul in the stomach—not with any great force but enough to wind Paul and throw him off-balance. Paul fell back but rolled easily and came up ready for the next assault.

There wasn't one. Vogel was already disappearing through the bedroom door, slamming it shut behind him. Paul swore and sprang at the door, wrenching it open in time to see Vogel standing in the landing doorway, gun in hand. Paul lunged back just as Vogel fired; the bullet slammed into the wall, missing him by only inches.

Looking around quickly, he spotted his own gun lying beside the bed. He waited by the bedroom door, gun in hand and then dived through it, loosing off a shot at the landing doorway as he did so.

There was nobody there, although this did not surprise him at all. Vogel had disappeared. Paul was too winded even to think of pursuit.

He had lost him.

Paul swore, savagely, a vicious monosyllable of frustration. He had almost had him . . .

He took several deep breaths, regaining his self-control. He would have to leave soon—the noise of their struggle in the bedroom would have been heard and the police would probably be there in a matter of minutes but if there were any clues, he had to find them.

Vogel had clearly been through the flat fairly thoroughly. It was pointless looking in the places he had already searched. Paul's eyes suddenly came to rest on the handbag lying next to the bed.

He rummaged through its contents. There was the usual paraphernalia but Paul was only interested in the scraps of paper—receipts, bills, bus tickets, anything.

He picked out a slip of paper; on it was written train departure times from Waterloo Station. To "Rock", it looked

like. Rock? Paul looked closer. No, not "Rock", but "Roch".
Rochdale? Rochester?

Suddenly, Paul sat back. There it was. Rochester. Next
door to Chatham, where Vogel had spent two years before
the war, reporting on naval activity. A town he undoubtedly
knew well.

Coincidence? Possibly, but why would Maureen Riordan
have wanted to go to Rochester? On the other hand, if Vogel
was going to make a kill, wouldn't he do it on familiar
territory, if he could?

Paul was in the act of pocketing the slip of paper when he
realised his folly. He didn't want to hide Vogel's destination
from the British; far from it. They stood a far better chance of
stopping Vogel than he did. It might not be his finger that
pulled the trigger if they caught him but it would be almost as
good knowing he had trapped Vogel . . .

He found a pen on the dressing table and began to write on
the slip of paper.

CHAPTER 9

Tyler looked at his watch; it was nearly time. He stared at the telephone, willing it to ring. Would 'Paul' keep his word or had the message just been a red herring?

He rubbed his eyes. When had he last had a good night's sleep? Five days ago? Six? Too long, anyway . . . He realised Randall was staring curiously at him.

"Reckon he'll phone, sir?"

"God only knows. He said he would in that note."

"If we can believe it."

"True. Very true." Tyler could still remember his own feelings of disbelief when he had read the message left on the slip of paper in the Riordan girl's flat. This man 'Paul' had claimed that he had been sent to protect the King's life and that he wanted Vogel stopped just as much as M15 did. He had drawn attention to the 'Roch' at the top of the paper, saying that he believed it referred to Rochester and had finished off with the information that he assumed that his telephone contact was blown; he would therefore be calling that number at twelve fifty-five exactly to give them a further message. Fenton had been frankly disbelieving when Tyler had shown him the note; he was convinced that it was a disinformation ploy. Tyler was not so sure; it corroborated Lorenz's story completely. Yet, whether he believed the note or not, there was little he could do but go along with it; 'Paul' had disappeared without trace . . .

He stood up and began to prowl around, restlessly. 'Lynx' had lived in a dingy two-room flat with peeling wallpaper and a large damp patch behind the chest of drawers. They had found a radio in a suitcase hidden under the floorboards in the bedroom; clearly, he had been able to communicate directly with Germany. How long had he been operating? wondered Tyler. He had moved into the flat two months before but where had he been before that? Had he been travelling around the country for months or years, never staying long in one place, or had he only arrived in England eight weeks ago? How long had he been living in places like this, waiting for that knock on the door? Tyler knew that he would never know the answer to those questions now . . .

The phone rang: Tyler snatched it up. "Hallo?" He gestured to Randall, who nodded and spoke into a microphone.

"This is Paul. I assume you got my message." The English was fluent, idiomatic and with no trace of a foreign accent.

"Yes, we did, Paul." Tyler saw Randall nod; the Post Office technicians were trying to trace the call. "You said you would tell us more today."

"Don't try to keep me talking," said the voice, curtly. "You'll find another message in a Left Luggage Locker. I'll tell you where in a moment. What is your name?"

"Pardon?" Tyler had heard the question; he was still stalling for time.

"You heard. I shall hang up if you try that again."

"Tyler."

"Right. If I have any further messages, I'll use this number. You can find my message in Left Luggage Locker number 74 at St. Pancras Station." The line went dead.

Tyler cursed and slammed the 'phone down. He shouted to Randall, "I'm taking the car. It'll take me about 20 minutes. Get on the 'phone and get a squad of men round to St. Pancras Station immediately. Left Luggage Locker number 74."

WATERLOO STATION.

Paul replaced the telephone and left the phone booth. He looked up at the large station clock; the Rochester train would be leaving any minute. He picked up his suitcase and walked unhurriedly to where the train was waiting. He had no doubt that within minutes a horde of police and security agents would be descending on St. Pancras Station; but in the meantime he would be on his way out of London. They would find the message he had left; whether they believed him was another matter.

He had left a second message that morning, one addressed to Carolyn that he had sealed in an envelope and placed on the mantelpiece before he had gone out. He felt guilty that he had not even told her face to face that he was going away; he had explained in the letter that his office had sent him up to Liverpool on urgent business and he would be away for some time. He owed her some sort of explanation for his sudden disappearance; but he knew that at least part of the reason he had left her a note was to prevent her becoming suspicious. And it had been the coward's way out. He was not proud of the way he had behaved . . .

Perhaps it had been for the best after all, he told himself as he boarded the train. It had been impossible right from the start; it was better to end it this way. She would soon forget him.

Whether he would ever forget her was another matter . . .

WHITEHALL.

Fenton came into the room dead on the stroke of ten o'clock, nodded to the others sitting around the table and sat down. He called the meeting to order. There were only five men around the table, one of whom, Menzies, was looking distinctly ill at ease. Tyler, sitting opposite Menzies, was not at all surprised at this; it was his head on the block.

The others present were both from the Palace staff. Colonel Newton was in charge of the King's "bodyguard", although it was a strictly unofficial unit. The King had only accepted its presence at his public engagements with extreme reluctance; Newton's job was not an easy one at the best of times. Major Weldon, the other Palace representative, was one of His Majesty's A.D.Cs; he would present the King's views on the subject. It was he who spoke first in response to Fenton's nod.

"His Majesty has been informed of the situation and the

request for him to alter his itinerary has been made. His Majesty stated quite categorically that he would make no alterations at all and that his duty to his people came first. Nor would he consider moving to Sandringham or Balmoral."

"We thought as much," said Fenton, glumly. "His Majesty is a brave man . . ." He turned to Menzies. "Brigadier, have we been able to ascertain which documents Lockhart made available to Vogel?"

Menzies made a pathetic attempt at bluster. "There is no evidence that any documents at all were made available."

"Oh, come now," retorted Fenton. "He and his girlfriend have both been murdered within hours of each other and there is little doubt that Vogel was responsible."

"It could have been a jealous boyfriend—"

"Rubbish!" exploded Tyler. "They were both killed by a professional. The girl was strangled and the killer knew exactly where to exert pressure. Lockhart's neck was broken. Again, it was professionally done, take my word for it. Not a jealous boyfriend."

Menzies glared at Tyler, who seemed quite unabashed.

"The documents?" prompted Fenton, quietly.

"We have no way of knowing. None were actually removed."

"But they could have been copied," said Fenton patiently. "Which relevant documents did Lockhart peruse in the last three weeks?"

"Lockhart had access to all the files," said Menzies. "He wouldn't necessarily have booked them out, although he was very conscientious about that."

"You mean," said Tyler incredulously, "he could have taken out any file at all and nobody would have been any the wiser?"

"Well . . . yes," admitted Menzies. "But, as I said, Lockhart was very conscientious about that sort of thing."

"So conscientious he provided Vogel with information," muttered Tyler.

"We don't know he did!"

"Then why kill him?"

"Maybe because he refused to co-operate!"

"Then why kill the girl? Vogel had got what he wanted, so they were of no use to him any more."

"You say 'they'," interrupted Weldon. "I don't really see what part the girl played."

"It's the oldest trick in the book," explained Fenton. "We know that Lockhart has only been seeing this girl for a matter of weeks at most. It's what we call a 'honey trap'. Seduce the victim, produce compromising photographs and/or wire recordings and then blackmail him. It's widely used. Vogel evidently recruited the girl and used her as the bait."

"There's still no proof," protested Menzies.

"Agreed," said Fenton, curtly. "But we cannot afford to assume otherwise. We know Vogel is out to kill His Majesty. Lockhart had access to the information he needed. A stunningly beautiful young woman suddenly appears on the scene, throwing herself at Lockhart and then both are murdered on the same evening by a professional. Need I say more? We have to assume the worst—that Lockhart did indeed provide Vogel with the information he required."

"Yes, I see your point," said Menzies, partly mollified. "Assuming that Lockhart only saw the documents he actually booked out—" he glanced at Tyler, half-expecting a comment but Tyler said nothing—"then we still have a long list of documents. However—" he hesitated.

"Yes?" prompted Fenton.

"One batch might be significant. He booked it out five days ago for no apparent reason, although that is not to say that there was no reason—"

"Oh, get on with it," muttered Tyler.

Menzies decided to ignore Tyler's comment. "—however, Miss Waters, one of our typists, did notice that Lockhart seemed quite agitated when she took this batch of documents to him."

Tyler opened his mouth to ask the obvious question but then, as if realising that he was the wrong man to ask it, changed his mind and looked at Fenton.

As if on cue, Fenton said, "And those documents?"

"They contained the itineraries of various VIPs," said Menzies, slowly. Then, even more slowly, "Including His Majesty's itineraries for the next four weeks."

Nobody said anything for a full minute. It was Fenton who broke the silence.

"Thank you, Brigadier. I don't think we need detain you any further." It was a curt dismissal, thinly disguised.

Menzies nodded in defeat. He rose slowly and walked towards the door.

Tyler actually found himself feeling sorry for Menzies as he watched him leave. It had not been his fault, really. He had been given a nice, cosy desk job because he had influence in the right places and had not really taken it seriously, any more than anyone else had. He had allowed security, never very tight in the first place, to become lax. There had been no effective vetting of his subordinates, no secure procedures to restrict access to documents. He had been negligent, admittedly, but then nobody had really thought that something like this could possibly happen, not even the professionals. It was Menzies' misfortune that he would be made the scapegoat. Really, we're all to blame, thought Tyler.

Fenton turned to Newton. "What measures have you taken, Colonel?"

"I've had more men drafted into my unit. We'll be instituting house to house searches in the immediate areas. Marksmen on rooftops. Having His Majesty's entourage consisting of tall men for extra protection. Explosives experts. I know that we've been told that Roeder is a marksman but I'm not taking any chances—they could use a bomb. My men will be instructed to shoot on sight and to shoot to kill."

"Not much else you can do," said Fenton. "Which brings us to the next point. How much weight do we attach to this message we received from 'Paul'?"

Newton gave a derisive snort. "Very little, I should imagine."

"Why?" asked Tyler, bluntly.

"There's absolutely no reason to believe it's genuine!"

Newton protested. "The idea that the Germans have sent over a team to protect the King is ludicrous!"

"That's precisely why I'm prepared to consider that possibility," said Tyler levelly. "If they wanted a ploy to throw us off the scent, wouldn't they have chosen something less outrageous?"

"Go on, Tyler," said Weldon. "I take it you've got more than just a hunch about this?"

"I think I have, yes. Firstly, we know there are two groups in England at the moment. Secondly, we've got Lorenz's statement, which he's sticking to through thick and thin and which is being borne out by what Paul has told us. And we know that there is an Anti-Hitler Conspiracy active in Germany. What I am saying is this: the idea is not without substance."

"Still pretty unbelievable, though," said Weldon.

"Well, we've also got the question of what happened in the Riordan girl's flat. I'd say Vogel killed the girl but was surprised by Paul—that's when the shots were fired. They were from two different guns, remember. Paul left us the note drawing our attention to Rochester—which is on the King's schedule. And the message he left at St. Pancras gave his reasons for believing that was where Vogel would make the attempt. Apparently, Vogel knows the area well. Everything Paul has said and done ties in with what Lorenz has told us."

"On the other hand, it could still be an elaborate deception," said Fenton. He held up his hand to forestall Tyler's protest. "No, hear me out, Tyler. You yourself said that this message from the Abwehr could have been a ruse to distract attention from the real killers—Paul's group. And let me remind you that we only have Lorenz's word that he and Paul are the only members of this group. Why didn't the Abwehr message inform us of Paul's mission?

"Paul could have engineered the entire situation to make us concentrate on Rochester, while he or Vogel carries out the assassination attempt elsewhere. We can be reasonably certain that they have obtained details of the King's itinerary; they could choose any of his engagements."

"But what about the fight in the flat?"

"It could have been staged and the note left to lead us the wrong way."

Tyler shook his head. "It's too elaborate. Why go to all this trouble just to draw attention to Rochester? They must know that we would still maintain maximum security precautions at all of the King's visits; we wouldn't concentrate on Rochester to the exclusion of all else. And why tell us what the objective of their operation is anyway? No, I don't think they'd go to such extravagant lengths."

"Unless the operation has another objective entirely. Who knows what Vogel is doing at the moment? Or Paul, come to that?" Fenton leaned forward. "All right, Tyler, I'll grant you that it's also difficult to believe that they'd go to such elaborate lengths for any operation but it's difficult to believe that the Germans would send in a group of agents to protect His Majesty. And without informing us they were doing it when they had the opportunity to do so. We cannot afford to take any chances at all. We are talking about His Majesty's life."

Tyler nodded slowly. Fenton was right, of course.

"Agreed," said Newton. "If this Paul shows himself anywhere near the King, I shall have no hesitation in ordering my men to shoot to kill."

ROCHESTER, KENT.

Vogel relaxed slightly as Roeder came down the rickety steps; the other man was a quarter of an hour late and if he had not appeared within the next five minutes Vogel would have abandoned the rendezvous. The meeting was taking place in the cellar of a bombed-out house, the only illumination being a flickering oil lamp hanging from the low ceiling. Vogel had found the ruined building the night before and had left a message at Rochester station instructing Roeder how to find it.

"Sorry I'm late," said Roeder. "It took me a while to find it."

"Never mind that. Put your suitcase over there."

"Did you bring the gun?"

"Yes, it's in a safe place."

"Is it still on for tomorrow?"

Vogel nodded. "It is. Now please pay close attention. The King will be arriving at about eleven a.m. at Rochester station. It is there that the assassination will take place." He placed a sketched diagram on the floor in front of Roeder and pointed to the various features in the drawing. "The main entrance has a forecourt. Opposite the station is a row of three storey office buildings. The distance from these to the station forecourt is about thirty metres."

"Too close," said Roeder. "First place they'd look after the shot. I wouldn't have time to get clear."

"Exactly. I want you positioned here." He indicated a row of buildings further along the street. "These are four storey buildings. They used to be Victorian town houses but they've been divided up into small flats now. This nearest one is about a hundred metres away. There is still a clear field of fire and the angle is such that the shot would still appear to come from the vicinity of these nearer buildings. They will search them first, which should give you ample time to get clear."

"Fair enough," said Roeder. A hundred metres, with the telescopic sight and the high-powered Mauser; there would be no problem. "Where will you be?"

Vogel hesitated momentarily. "I shall be in the vicinity. If for some reason you are unable to shoot then I will be in a position to carry out the assassination myself. You do not need to know the details." He ignored Roeder's look of resentment and continued:

"After the assassination has taken place, get out of those flats fast. Leave the gun behind. You should not have any trouble getting out if you remain calm. All the security forces will be running round in circles. They won't know where the shots came from in any case. Use the fire escape at the rear of the building or the rear exit. If you are challenged, act as though you are a resident who's coming to see what's going on—you heard all the screams and shouts.

"Once you get away, go to the Town Hall. Meet me outside there at noon. Make sure you're not followed, of course. We'll then proceed to our pick-up point and be back in Germany within twenty-four hours. Any questions?"

"What do I do if you're not at the Town Hall?"

Vogel nodded. He tore off a corner of the diagram and wrote down a number. "Phone this number and you'll be given instructions."

Roeder pocketed the scrap of paper. "Also—how do I get in to these flats without being spotted?"

"Leave all that to me. I'll get you and the gun in without anyone noticing you're there. All you will have to do is squeeze the trigger."

Roeder nodded. "No problem," he said, as though he scarcely needed Vogel's help. "So tomorrow we kill the King?" Vogel could sense the eager anticipation in the other man.

He nodded. "Tomorrow. At eleven o'clock. Give or take a few minutes."

CHAPTER 10

Vogel awoke instantly and looked around the dingy little bedroom. He glanced once at the girl sleeping beside him. Her name eluded him for the moment but he made no attempt to recall it; she had served her purpose, providing both sexual relief and a bed for the night. Vogel was not concerned by the fact that she would probably be able to identify him; in the extremely unlikely event of her being questioned, there was little she could tell the police. In any case, he would be back in Germany by then.

He had picked her up in a pub near the Town Hall; young enough to be fairly attractive but with far too much make-up. Their activities during the night had left him relaxed yet alert.

Vogel slipped silently out of bed and went into the tiny living room. His suitcase was still where he had left it, in the centre of the floor; he had told the girl he was a travelling salesman and that the case contained his samples. The explanation had been ignored; as long as he could pay, she couldn't really have cared less.

Inside the suitcase was a single change of clothing which Vogel ignored for the present, except to lift the trousers to take out a wooden case about eighteen inches long, a foot wide and four inches deep. He did not open it but placed it on the floor.

Reaching under the jacket, he took out a sheet of brown paper which he used to wrap the wooden case, tying it as a parcel with string taken from the suitcase. Next, he removed a flat metal case from the jacket pocket and took out a rubber stamp, which he pressed onto the parcel, deliberately smudging the imprint. Vogel then scrawled an illegible address on the parcel before replacing everything in the suitcase.

Whistling tunelessly, he went through into the bathroom to shave.

Vogel walked into Rochester station at a few minutes after eight, carrying a suitcase, and wandered over to the blackboard that gave details of the day's departures. Had anyone been observing his actions, it would have been obvious by his dismayed expression that the train he wanted was not due for some time. In fact, nobody noticed him at all.

He looked around indecisively for a few moments and then headed for the Left Luggage Office, where he deposited the suitcase, pocketing the claim ticket. Then he left, clearly in no hurry. The girl in the ticket office saw him go but promptly forgot all about him as she had to answer an enquiry from an eager child. Yes, it was true the King was coming to the station today.

The door to Number 37 opened as Joe Maynard came up the path. An attractive woman in her mid twenties stood in the doorway. "Morning, Mrs. Bell," he said, smiling as he handed over the envelope. "Looks like a bill, I'm afraid."

"It always is," said Mrs. Bell resignedly. She smiled invitingly at Maynard. "Fancy a cuppa, Joe?"

Maynard suppressed a smile. "I'm afraid not, Mrs. Bell. I've still got quite a lot of deliveries to make and I'm late as it is."

"Pity. Another time, perhaps?"

"Perhaps."

One of these days, Maynard promised himself as he made his way back down the path, one of these days I'll take her up on that offer and we'll see if she really means it or if she's just leading me on . . .

Maynard walked on down the street, oblivious of the dark-haired man who had been following him ever since he had left the sorting-office an hour before. As he turned into the alleyway that served as a short-cut, he was completely unaware that the other man was only a few yards behind him.

There was a sound behind him but before he could even begin to look round, an arm encircled his neck. The hand grabbed his jaw and yanked his head back. Maynard was looking into the sun, just about to cry out in surprise, when Vogel's right hand chopped into his throat just above the Adam's apple.

The sun was the last thing Joe Maynard ever saw.

Vogel looked around quickly. The alley itself was too exposed but there were allotments beyond the fence. Opening a gate, he saw a small shed with its door half open; it was clearly disused.

Grabbing Maynard under the armpits, he began to drag the body towards the gate. It had been a good, clean kill; no noise, no blood. It would not do to have bloodstains all over the uniform, of course; they would attract unwelcome attention.

It was going well.

Newton and his men arrived at the station at just after eight thirty. Although the King was not due until eleven, a crowd of onlookers was already beginning to form outside the station. They were always an added complication but the whole point of the visit was that the King would be seen by his subjects; the spectators were an integral part of the whole procedure. Newton's men would be dispersed throughout the crowd but they would not be watching His Majesty; they would be watching for any sudden attempt to produce something from a pocket or bag.

Newton stood in the station forecourt, looking around at the surrounding buildings and began to issue orders. "McIntyre, take your men and search those buildings. Usual story." He indicated the buildings opposite. "Cranston, take your lot and do those ones there." This time, he was referring to the group of buildings that Vogel had decided on.

Cranston was an ambitious Detective Sergeant, recently seconded to Special Branch, who knew that this assignment might well bring him promotion; he was keen to make a good impression. Dividing up his men into teams of two—one pair for each group of flats—he selected a morose-looking Detective Constable called Russell as his own partner. The two of them took the nearest building to the station.

They found the caretaker of the flats in a small cubby hole in the entrance lobby and Cranston gave him the cover story, that a man had been seen entering the premises during the night. Just a formality, but they had to see if there were any signs of a break-in.

One by one, they checked the flats, repeating the story to each occupant. Cranston came at last to Number 9, the uppermost flat. He knocked; a young woman with dark hair opened the door.

"Miss Pattison?" asked Cranston, consulting the list the caretaker had given him.

"Yes?"

Cranston showed her his identification card and went into his story, suspicious prowler, had she seen or heard anything, purely routine enquiry, and so on.

"No. I was fast asleep."

"Were you in all evening, Miss Pattison?"

"No, I'm on back shift—"

"You work in a factory?"

"Yes. Preston's. I'm on the late shift this week, so I don't usually get in until eleven."

"I see." Cranston made a note in his notebook. "Have you noticed anything missing?"

"Well, no." She seemed worried. "But, there again, I haven't checked."

"May I come in for a moment? He may have gained entrance to your flat, even if he didn't steal anything. I'd be able to tell if he had forced any locks, or picked them."

"Yes, certainly."

Cranston's search, as ever, was thorough. There was no sign of a gunman or a gun. Nothing untoward at all. "No need to worry at all, Miss Pattison. He certainly hasn't been here. Sorry to bother you."

The reports he received from the rest of his team a few minutes later were identical; there was no sign of any gunman. "Right," he told them. "I'll report back. But hang around and keep an eye on the flats. Don't let anyone in who looks remotely suspicious."

As he headed back towards the station, he half-noticed the postman on the far side of the road, repairing a puncture, his bicycle lying flat on the pavement. Although he had not noticed, the postman had been there when he had entered the flats. Cranston gave him a cursory glance and then forgot all about him.

Russell, meanwhile, went back into the flats and explained to the caretaker that they had reason to believe that the prowler would be back so they were keeping a watch on the flats for the time being.

The caretaker wasn't interested. He went back to his Agatha Christie novel.

Across the road, Vogel replaced the inner tube and squeezed the tyre back onto the wheel. As he pumped the tyre up, he watched Cranston walk back towards the station. They were certainly making thorough checks, that much was clear. Vogel had only decided on the postman disguise as a safety precaution; he had not anticipated that the security would be so tight. They were evidently taking no chances.

No matter. They had searched the flats and would be unlikely to do so again. He mounted the bicycle and cycled off, remembering in the nick of time to ride on the left. Leaving the bicycle in a deserted alleyway, he returned on foot; the bicycle might attract attention if he left it parked outside the flats.

Russell was in the caretaker's cubby-hole when Vogel pushed open the street door. The detective was bored. This was the third time they had been through this rigmarole and he suspected this wouldn't be the last. Russell was already fed up with it all, not having seen his girlfriend for over a week and, it seemed, for no good reason. When he saw the familiar postman's uniform, he thought nothing of it. Idly, he watched the postman going upstairs with a parcel under his arm and then returned to the pin-up magazine he had discovered in the desk. Within seconds, like Cranston before him, he had forgotten the postman.

On the top landing, Vogel took a parcel from the mailbag. He knocked at the door of Number 9 and heard somebody coming to the door. A young woman in factory overalls opened the door.

"Parcel for you, miss."

"Oh! I wasn't expecting anything."

Vogel gave her the parcel. "Mind, it's a bit heavy. Sorry. Silly of me. Almost forgot." He took a notebook and pencil out of his pocket. "Would you sign for it, please?"

The girl was holding the parcel in both hands and stared at the proffered pencil. "Oh. Yes. Just a minute." She turned round and carried the parcel into the living room, setting it on the sideboard. She did not hear Vogel following her into the flat; he had returned the pencil to the pocket and was now holding the stiletto knife in his right hand.

At the last moment, some instinct made her turn round. She opened her mouth to scream as she saw the knife but it was already stabbing towards her. There was a shaft of agony just below her ribs and the thought came that she had to scream now or it would be too late . . .

The blackness came first.

Vogel had stabbed upwards, the blade entering under the ribs and angled so that it pierced the heart; Death had been virtually instantaneous. Catching the girl as she began to fall, he lowered her carefully to the floor and then closed and locked the door. He removed the knife from the body and cleaned it carefully in the sink.

The body was lying in the middle of the room; he would have to move it out of the way, or Roeder would probably throw up at the sight of it. He dragged the corpse into the bedroom and closed the door on it. After looking quickly around the living room, Vogel left the door on the latch and walked off along the landing, whistling.

Descending the last flight of stairs he was relieved to see

that the two men were still in the cubby hole; it made the next part of the plan easier. He went up to the door and leaned through the gap. "Excuse me."

Russell and the caretaker looked up. "Yes?" said the caretaker.

"Does a Roger Lister live here?"

The caretaker shook his head. "Never heard of him, mate."

"That's all I need," Vogel said disgustedly, reaching into the postbag and taking out a bulky envelope. "It's just that this is for him and it's got this address on it. Looks important."

"Can't 'elp you, mate. He don't live 'ere."

"Bloody typical," Vogel grumbled, producing a packet of cigarettes. "This is always happening to me. Either of you want a fag?"

"Cheers, mate," said the caretaker. Both he and Russell took one. Russell produced a box of matches and lit the cigarettes; as he leaned forward to take the light, Vogel saw the pin-up magazine on Russell's lap.

"Mind if I have a quick look? Hey—look at that pair."

Vogel was now almost entirely obscuring their view of the lobby and so neither man saw Roeder slip past the cubby hole and run silently up the stairs.

He pushed open the door of the uppermost flat and closed it behind him, locking it. There was a patch of blood on the carpet; he looked hurriedly away and went over to the parcel on the sideboard.

Roeder unwrapped the package, which was the one Vogel had prepared at the prostitute's flat that morning, and opened the wooden case within. Inside were the various components of a high-velocity rifle and a telescopic lens, carefully packed in cotton wool, just as carefully oiled and greased.

Almost lovingly, he began to assemble the rifle, whistling tunelessly to himself.

Newton had made his preparations. The spectators were to be

kept ouside the station behind a cordon some thirty yards from the station entrance. Thus, a shot from a handgun would be difficult although not impossible. Privately, Newton doubted that the assassin would attempt anything from such close range but he was taking no chances, especially with the steadily growing crowd that was gathering outside.

The toilets had been searched to see if anyone was hiding inside, as well as the station offices. The Left Luggage Office had also been searched but not very closely. The luggage itself was not checked; the office was too far from the platform the King was using to present a serious threat as regards a bomb attack. The search had merely been to see if anyone was in hiding: it was clean.

It never occurred to anyone to maintain a watch on the Left Luggage Office.

Cranston reported back to Newton. "Nothing, sir. We've checked every flat or office that overlooks the station within rifle range. Nothing at all."

Newton nodded. "Very well, Sergeant. You've got the buildings under surveillance?"

"Yes, sir. Nobody can go in or out of any of them without being questioned."

"Good. Keep me in touch if anything develops."

"Yes, sir."

Newton glanced at his watch. There was still an hour to go. He walked impatiently to and fro in the forecourt, barely noticing the tall man who was showing his documents to a young private. Vogel was passed through after a search that surprised him by its thoroughness. There was no doubt about it; something had alerted the British. They were expecting trouble; the question was whether they knew precisely what was being planned.

There was a possibility that they had deduced that an assassination attempt was to be made; they might have come to the correct conclusions regarding Lockhart's murder. Or Koenig might have tipped them off; Vogel had little doubt that Koenig had been sent to England to prevent the assassination. There was no other explanation for his presence in the girl's flat.

Not that it made any difference to the assassination attempt; that would still go ahead. Roeder was safely in place now and would carry out the shooting. Of course, he would be unlikely to escape, but he was never intended to. Vogel had no intention of meeting him at the Town Hall; by then, he would be on his way to the pick up point on the Essex coast. Roeder would be left stranded—the telephone number Vogel had given him was fictitious—and would not be able to tell the British where Vogel was. The British would get his description from him, of course, but that would be of little use to them; Vogel would be back in Germany long before they picked up his trail. There was no reason why the operation should not proceed . . .

Vogel arrived at the Left Luggage Office, checking carefully for any sign of surveillance. There was none; the British were clearly expecting a long-range rifle attempt or, failing that, an attack outside the station. Obviously, they felt that an assassin would be less likely to make his attempt inside the station, where his chances of escape were considerably reduced. In fact, Vogel agreed with them; he was not entirely happy with the prospect, should it become necessary, but that was why he had decided to do exactly that—it was so improbable. In any case, he estimated that with the Schmeisser machine-pistol that was concealed in the suitcase, he had an even chance of shooting his way out if he had to, with the help of the grenades and smoke canisters that were also part of the "luggage".

He collected the suitcase and walked towards the nearest platform seats.

Paul realised that today was the day as soon as he saw Newton's unit arrive. They were out in force, checking the nearby roofs and buildings and stopping everyone entering or leaving the station. Somehow, he had to get inside the station, for that was where he was sure Vogel would be. Roeder would be their first line of attack but if that failed, Vogel would be inside the station, ready to take advantage of any confusion created by Roeder's shots.

So he, Paul, had to get inside the station. Easier said than done, as he wanted to get in armed—and the soldiers at the entrance were searching anybody who looked remotely suspicious. Paul walked slowly towards the station, watching the bustling activity, paying particular attention to the soldiers. Almost certainly, extra troops would have been drafted in and it was these troops he was trying to spot. They would be less experienced and easier to trick; the ones who had to be told what to do, rather than those who already knew.

He soon spotted an ideal victim; the soldier was still in his teens and looked very keen to do well. Too keen, Paul hoped, as he waited for the approaching soldier at the entrance to a short alley, apparently staring intently into it. He turned and beckoned urgently to the soldier who hesitated and then came running over.

"I thought I saw someone dive into this alley, like he was trying to avoid you lot."

"Did you?" The private's eyes flickered to the alley, then back. "You sure?"

"Yes—there he is!"

"Where?"

"Behind the dustbins—see him?" Paul was pointing insistently with his right hand, his left on the soldier's arm, pushing him into the alley. The private fell for it and walked cautiously into the alley, rifle at the ready.

"I think I saw him going through the gate." There was a wooden door in the alley wall, some six feet high or so. Paul was ready to give him an encouraging push if necessary but there was no need; the soldier was already trotting down the passageway.

The door was partly open. The private hesitated then, releasing the safety catch on his rifle, pushed the door open with his foot. Inside was the garden of a bombed-out house. As the soldier entered, he saw an Anderson shelter to his left, the door suspiciously open.

The young private approached it cautiously, unaware that Paul was two feet behind him, following stealthily. The recruit paused at the entrance, looking into the gloomy interior.

Paul's hand chopped into the back of the soldier's neck. The soldier pitched forward, unconscious. Paul dragged him into the shelter, pulling the door shut behind him and began to undress the soldier.

Minutes later, he left the shelter clad in the uniform of a British Army private. It was a little on the small side but not drastically so; it was unlikely that anybody would pass comment on it. He closed the door as he left. The luckless soldier would be unconscious for several hours yet and was unlikely to be discovered by accident; the house was derelict and its shelter had not been used for some time.

Paul stepped briskly out of the alley.

"Oy, you, soldier!" came the voice behind him.

Paul froze momentarily and then turned round. A burly, impatient looking sergeant was striding towards him.

"Yes, Sarge?"

"You checked down there?" He gestured at the alley.

"Yes, Sarge. All clear."

"Right. You'd better report back to Sergeant Ellis, then."

"Right, Sarge."

Breathing a sigh of relief, Paul blessed the fact that when new men were drafted into a unit, nobody was able to spot a strange face; the old-timers would assume he was a new boy and vice versa. In any case, the uniform dispelled all doubts.

Two minutes later, Paul was inside the station.

Tyler reached the station in a boiling temper at a few minutes to eleven. The car bringing Fenton, Randall and himself had broken down at Bexleyheath and had eventually had to be replaced but the delay meant that they had arrived only minutes before the King.

Newton was in the station forecourt. Tyler looked at the buildings opposite. These would be the ones under the most intense surveillance. As soon as anybody appeared at a window with anything that looked remotely like a rifle, he would be centred in the crosshairs of a telescopic sight himself.

Tyler studied the Victorian buildings further away. These would be not so closely watched and so there would be a better chance of escaping. It was a greater distance to shoot but no great problem for a marksman. If he were organising it, that's where he'd put the sniper . . .

"I'll have a nose round, if I may," he said to Newton.

"Help yourself," replied Newton curtly.

Tyler walked away, concealing his irritation.

Behind him, in the station, he could hear the train coming in.

Gradually, the train came to a halt, the royal carriage coming to rest alongside the red carpet where the Lord Mayor and various local dignitaries waited to greet His Majesty. Apart from them, the platform was deserted; even the railway staff had been ushered away by Newton's men, much to their annoyance.

There was a pause and then the carriage door opened. The King stepped down. If he was surprised by the deserted platform, he showed no sign as he walked forward to shake hands with the Lord Mayor.

Platform 1 had been cleared, but not the others. There were very few waiting passengers and their view would be obscured by the royal train in any case. Nobody took much notice of the man sitting on a bench on Platform 3.

Tyler flashed his identification pass at Cranston when the latter challenged him from the cubby-hole where he was sitting with Russell. "You searched the flats?" Tyler began.

"Er—yes," Cranston replied, taken aback.

"Anybody been in or out since then?"

Cranston looked at Russell, who answered, "No. Nobody."

"You're sure of that?"

"Positive. I've been here all the while. Nobody. Well— only the postman."

"Postman?" said Cranston suddenly, as a chord of memory was struck. "The one who was fixing a puncture over the road?"

"I suppose so."

"When was this?" asked Tyler.

Cranston shrugged. "While we searched the flats. I noticed him when I came out."

So he had been around to see the search, thought Tyler. Oh, don't be so damned silly, he told himself. It's only a postman.

But it might not be.

He turned back to Russell. "Did you see him leave?"

"Yes. A couple of minutes later."

"Did you see what he was delivering?"

"Yes. He was carrying a parcel."

Perfectly normal, thought Tyler; delivering a parcel. What you'd expect to see a postman doing.

What you'd expect to see.

Who notices the postman? thought Tyler, feeling a sudden hollow sensation in the pit of his stomach.

"What size was it, the parcel?"

Russell shrugged. "About two feet by one."

"Oh no . . ." Tyler breathed.

"What—" began Cranston, but Tyler was already sprinting for the stairs. After a moment's hesitation, Cranston followed him.

The King finished talking to the dignitaries and then walked through the station entrance into the sunlight. At once, there was a deafening cheer from the crowd gathered outside. The King smiled and waved to them, making no comment on the fact that the spectators were cordoned off a good thirty yards away . . .

Roeder had seen the train arrive and moved the rifle into

position, taking care that the barrel did not protrude through the open window. It was therefore invisible from the street below. Through the telescopic sight, he could see every detail of the station entrance and forecourt. He adjusted the focus slightly, aiming at a soldier standing by the entrance. The focus was perfect. He centred the crosshairs on the man's forehead. Right between the eyes.

"Bang!" he whispered. He felt completely relaxed, confident. He would not miss.

There was a pause during which, Roeder assumed, the King was talking to the local VIPs and then there was a movement in the entrance. A group of men emerged into the sunlight. The first three were all tall, powerfully built men who scanned the windows and rooftops opposite. They were obviously bodyguards—and looking in the wrong place.

Roeder moved the sights slightly and the unmistakeable figure of the King came into view. Roeder lined up the crosshairs, once again aiming at the centre of the forehead. It was going to be so easy . . .

His finger began to squeeze the trigger . . .

Tyler was slowed down by his limp so that Cranston passed him on the first landing. By the time they reached the top flat, Cranston was about three yards ahead of him.

Cranston had already come to the same conclusion as Tyler, that the uppermost flat would offer the best view of the forecourt and so he drew his gun as he reached the top landing. Behind him, Tyler did the same.

Cranston tried the door. It was locked. He hesitated, but only for an instant. He aimed the gun at the lock and fired.

Roeder's finger began to tighten on the trigger and then he paused. Perhaps he ought to aim at the chest and be more certain of a hit? He dismissed the thought and mentally cursed himself for the hesitation. He had considered the alternatives long before and he had decided then, so why waste time now?

While he had delayed, the King had moved out of the

sights. Roeder centred the crosshairs once more and again began to squeeze the trigger . . .

He froze.

Someone was trying the door.

The crash of a gunshot sent Roeder into explosive action. He leaped up from his crouching position by the window and spun round as Cranston kicked the door open.

Cranston dropped immediately into a pistol shooting crouch but as he brought his gun up he knew he was too late, a lifetime too late . . . the rifle was already pointing straight at him . . .

Roeder fired from the hip and the bullet took Cranston in the chest, hurling him back across the corridor to smash into the opposite wall, arms outflung. He slid slowly to the floor, already dead.

Tyler did not spare him a glance. He dived forward and rolled once, so that he was lying full length on his stomach in the doorway facing into the flat. Roeder reacted very quickly; the rifle was aimed too high, but was already sweeping downwards when Tyler fired, rolling convulsively to one side and to his feet in one movement.

Roeder reeled back, hit in the left shoulder. He slammed into the wall next to the window, fighting desperately to retain his balance. Tyler came hurtling through the door, firing a second time, before diving off to his left behind the sofa. Roeder gasped in pain as the bullet tore into his left arm, but squeezed off a rapid shot, one-handed. The shot ploughed into the sofa's upholstery but Roeder had already traversed the barrel, aiming to the right of the sofa, where Tyler's momentum would take him.

Roeder had guessed wrong. Tyler rolled into view on the sofa's left hand side. Desperately, ignoring the agony in his left shoulder and arm, Roeder swung the rifle back and fired a split second before Tyler. But pain and fear had hurried Roeder's shot—the bullet slammed into the wall above Tyler's head.

Tyler's shot was carefully placed and slammed into Roeder's chest, pinning him momentarily to the wall, before he slowly toppled over and crashed heavily to the floor. He shuddered convulsively and then lay very still, his eyes staring sightlessly at the bloodstained rug.

The gunfire was heard at the station quite clearly. There was a momentary hush in the crowd and then a sudden hubbub of noise. Newton reacted immediately.

"Back into the station, sir!"

The King looked quizzically at him. "Are you giving me orders, Colonel? he asked, a trace of a smile on his face.

"Yes, Your Majesty, I am," said Newton, defiantly.

The King gestured at the crowd. "And what of them? What will they think?"

The spectators were milling around in confusion. Newton saw what the King meant; if they were to see him retreating into the station at this point, many would realise what was happening. There would be panic, hysteria.

The King saved the situation. Clearly unruffled, he waved again to the crowds, smiling broadly. To Newton's horror, he jumped up onto a small crate and began to speak to the crowd. He was a sitting target, for God's sake! thought Newton. They couldn't miss him like that! And he knew it, Newton realised. Yet he was doing it anyway. It was the bravest thing he had ever seen . . .

The speech was short; it was no more than a conventional patriotic exhortation, but the mere fact that the words were spoken calmed the crowd down. As he finished speaking, there was an outburst of cheering. He stepped down from the crate and walked unhurriedly back into the station as though nothing untoward had occured.

Behind him, Newton took what seemed to be his first breath for several minutes.

Paul saw the King as he re-entered the station and began to look around, trying to spot Vogel. There was no sign of him. Surely he would have to strike soon or the security units would be re-organised and ready to cope with a fresh emergency. So where was he?

He could see a tall Colonel coming through the entrance; he appeared to be in charge of security. The King, surrounded by six or seven men, had walked a little way down the platform. He seemed totally unconcerned. There was still no sign of Vogel. Perhaps he had been wrong. Perhaps there was no contingency plan. Perhaps—

"Don't move, friend." Paul froze at the voice from behind him.

"Turn round, slowly." Paul did so. He recognised the speaker immediately. It was the man who had tried to detain him at the park gates, six days before. Clearly, the man had recognised him as well and was taking no chances; he was holding a gun aimed unwaveringly at Paul's heart.

"Now drop your rifle."

Paul did so, trying not to show his numbing despair.

Randall had only spotted Paul by pure chance. He had been checking the waiting-room when he had heard the distant gunshots. He had been heading towards the main entrance when he had noticed the tall soldier standing on the platform, looking intently around.

Recognition came instantly.

Now, as the other man dropped his rifle, Randall beckoned to Fenton, who came over.

"What is it, Randall?"

"This is the one that got away from us at Hyde Park."

"Is he, indeed?" Fenton studied Paul as though he were a zoologist examining a new species.

"Listen," said Paul tersely. "You've got it all wrong. I command the group to which Lorenz belongs. You know Lorenz?"

"I may do," Fenton replied, noncommittally.

"If you do, then you'll know who I am. I am 'Paul'. You're looking for Vogel. So am I. I want to protect the King, not kill him."

"I find that hard to believe."

"Then why haven't I shot him already? I had a rifle and I

164

could hardly miss from here, could I? Would I be standing in full view of everybody if I wanted to kill him?"

Fenton rubbed his jaw, thoughtfully. It was undeniably true that the other man's actions were hardly consistent with those of a would-be assassin, but all the same—

Suddenly, Paul shouted out, "Look! Up there, on the bridge!"

Randall made no move to turn. "That's the oldest trick—" He got no further than that. Paul's hand chopped down on Randall's right wrist, knocking the gun to one side and paralysing the hand. The gun fell from Randall's nerveless fingers but even before it hit the ground, Paul had hooked his foot round Randall's leg. With a convulsive heave, Paul sent Randall reeling backwards, his outstretched arm knocking into Fenton, causing him to stumble as well.

Paul flicked a glance up at the bridge; Vogel was already raising the Schmeisser to its firing position. He had only seconds left . . .

Vogel did not hear the gunfire, but he saw the results when the King and his escort returned into the station. Roeder had missed; there was no time to wonder why or how. He picked up his suitcase and made his way along the platform to the footbridge staircase. Vogel watched the King's party as they came into view. They would be at a range of no more than thirty-five yards. At that range, he could hardly miss.

Vogel felt a momentary hesitation. As soon as he opened fire, he would betray his own presence. He had already worked out his escape route, but Vogel estimated his chances of survival as being no more than even. He could still turn back, just walk out of the smaller exit and disappear. He would probably not be questioned—the guards would be more concerned with people coming in than in those leaving. In that situation, the chances were better than ninety per cent for survival, he estimated.

To hell with it, he thought. He was so close. He had achieved the almost impossible; to back out now would be to withdraw from the coup of the war. It was totally irrational, of course, but he would see it through out of sheer stinking pride. Only he could have got this far, he told himself, and he couldn't back out now . . .

He put his suitcase down, opened it and took out the machine-pistol. He would deliver a withering burst of fire that would rake the platform where the King stood. Accuracy would not be essential, although he was a good marksman. There was no way that the King could escape the hail of bullets.

As Vogel lifted the Schmeisser into position, he noticed somebody running along the platform below, towards the King. It was Koenig . . .

He opened fire.

Paul sprinted along the platform, yelling, "He's up there! On the bridge!"

The last part of his shout was lost in the blast of a whistle from the locomotive. Behind him, Randall picked himself up and retrieved his gun. He had to hold it left-handed; his right was still paralysed. He lined up the gun on Paul's running figure but then hesitated; he was shooting with the wrong hand and the King was in the line of fire . . .

Fenton's voice cut through the confusion. "On the bridge, Randall! He's right!"

Randall looked up then and saw the figure on the footbridge, saw the machine-pistol already lining up on the King.

"Oh, sweet Jesus!" he whispered.

The group of men around the King saw an unarmed British soldier pelting towards them, gesturing frantically up at the bridge. They looked up and saw Vogel at the same moment as Randall. Like him, they froze for an instant.

In that moment, Paul hurtled through the King's protective ring of men. About four yards beyond the King was a pile of crates, the only cover within reach. Paul tried to recall the games of rugby he had played at Oxford so many years before and leaned forward in his run.

He cannoned into the King and took him with him, the force of his rush knocking the King backwards. Paul's arms wrapped themselves around him under the armpits, holding him up, until he virtually threw the King behind the crates, diving on top of him as the Schmeisser opened up.

Vogel mercilessly raked the platform in a five-second burst but he already knew instinctively that Faust had been unharmed. Most of the bodyguards were lying dead or wounded now, cut down by the machine-pistol but Koenig had almost certainly saved the King's life. Damn him! thought Vogel viciously.

His hand closed over one of the grenades in the suitcase and then hesitated. The platform's overhanging roof would intercept the trajectory of a lobbed grenade; it would have to be thrown in fast and flat to pass under the roof but still clear the crates. However, the grenade would then land some distance beyond the crates and would be unlikely to be close enough to kill the King when it detonated. In addition, Vogel would have to stand up to make the throw; he would be a sitting target.

No. The odds were too unfavourable. Perhaps one of the SS fanatics, willing to die for the Führer would have attempted it and just might have succeeded, but Vogel was not willing to die for anybody. He was not interested in suicidal heroics. He had lost; now he had to make his escape.

Reaching down into the suitcase, he turned a dial set onto several sticks of explosive before scooping up the grenades and smoke canisters, which he stuffed into his pockets. He fired a burst at the soldiers who had just erupted through the station entrance and pelted along the bridge, less than twenty seconds after he had originally opened fire. Vogel dropped a smoke canister as he left.

Six soldiers went bounding up the footbridge stairs in pursuit. The leading man, a young corporal, could see the spreading smokescreen ahead of him and hesitated, not knowing what lay beyond it but, telling himself that the German's only thought would be to escape rather than to lie in wait, he plunged on into the thick smoke.

He had gone only two yards or so when he tripped over the suitcase. He cried out in surprise and terror as he realised what was going to happen.

The explosives detonated directly below his falling body, killing him instantly. The explosive devices were designed to send shrapnel hurtling outwards from the blast; they were lethal at close range. Of the corporal's five companions, all but one were killed within a second, one being flung over the side of the bridge to land on the rails below.

The sixth man was found, minutes later, with both legs blown off just above the knee. He died before he reached hospital.

Vogel was descending the stairs two or three at a time when he heard the explosion. Two soldiers appeared at the foot of the stairway; both were cut down before they could even raise their guns.

On reaching the platform, Vogel lobbed a grenade at the small northern exit and then dropped a second smoke canister to cover his escape as he pelted along the platform towards the marshalling yards.

Following the blast of the grenade, there was comparative quiet in the station for a few seconds. Nobody knew for certain what was happening. The explosion at the southern end of the bridge, followed by a second blast only seconds later at the northern entrance had had their desired effect; they had created a state of utter confusion. Just what was going on? Was the King safe?

Randall was the exception. He had emerged from under the train on the opposite side to the platform and was thus in a position to see Vogel as he raced towards the marshalling yards. Without hesitation, he began to pursue him, running along the tracks, gun in hand.

Paul clambered gingerly to his feet as the firing died away. The King was also picking himself himself up, slowly.

"Are you all right, sir?"

"Yes, perfectly, thank you." He looked across at Paul and

forced a smile. "Rather unconventional, but I think I owe you my life, Private—?"

"Keen. Paul Keen, sir."

The King rose slowly to his feet, and shook Paul's hand. "Once again, thank you, Private Keen. I owe you a great deal."

Paul smiled, embarrassed, and looked away across the station. As he did so, he saw Vogel sprinting along the far platform. As far as he could see, there were no signs of anyone in pursuit.

"Excuse me, sir!"

He looked quickly around and scooped up a Sten gun from one of the dead soldiers on the platform. He leaped down onto the tracks and headed off in pursuit. He was not going to let Vogel escape again . . .

As he reached the marshalling yard, Paul saw Randall about twenty yards ahead of him.

"Randall!"

The other man spun round, gun at the ready. He saw who it was, hesitated briefly and then relaxed; he could hardly doubt Paul's story now. "Yes?" he answered.

"He's heading for the perimeter fence!"

"Right!" Randall moved off in the indicated direction, using the stationary wagons as cover, flitting between them, followed closely by Paul.

An explosion ahead of them sent them both diving instinctively for cover. Paul rose first and peered cautiously around a coal wagon. "He's blown a hole in the fence!"

Beyond the gaping hole were derelict buildings, half destroyed by bombs. Randall cursed softly. It was a good place to hide. He scanned the deserted site; there was no sign of Vogel.

"Could be a ruse," he mused. "It's a fairly obvious pointer to where he's gone, isn't it?"

"Yes, but I think he'll be wanting to get away as quickly as possible," replied Paul. "He won't want to be trapped inside the fence. I'd say that's where he's gone."

Randall made up his mind. If the German was still inside

the yard, then he could be dealt with by Newton's men but if he was through the fence, he and Paul were the only ones placed to cut him off. He went through the gap in a low, crouching run with Paul close behind. They sprawled full-length behind a pile of rubble.

"Nobody at home?" said Randall.

"Could be."

Randall glanced back the way they had come. A lone soldier had appeared at the gap in the fence.

"Corporal! Search inside the fence! We'll search the ruins!"

"Yes, sir."

Randall glanced at Paul and, without another word, leaped to his feet. He began to move further into the ruins, darting from cover to cover. Paul followed suit but headed off at a tangent; they had to cover as much ground as possible. They soon lost sight of the fence.

It was Paul who found Vogel. Moving rapidly from a low wall to the remains of a buttress, he saw him crouched behind another wall about twenty yards away. Paul dived for cover, just as Vogel twisted around and fired a short burst at him, the bullets passing only just above him.

Randall heard the gunfire and saw Vogel about thirty yards away. He fired and then jumped into cover himself.

Cautiously, Paul peered over the top of a pile of rubble. Vogel was nowhere to be seen. He could see Randall, his back flattened against a ruined wall, gun in hand. He gestured to Paul, indicating that he was going to move round behind Vogel. He would want covering fire; Paul raised a hand in acknowledgement.

Randall nodded. Paul fired a short burst over the top of the rubble as Randall scrambled across a ten yard gap to a low wall. Grinning, he gave a thumbs-up sign to Paul.

Vogel threw a stick grenade; Paul watched horror-struck as it arced through the air towards Randall. He opened his mouth to call out a warning but then ducked as Vogel's machine pistol swung round towards him.

The grenade dropped behind Randall and detonated less

than six feet from him. The blast lifted him bodily and flung him over the low wall. He hit the ground and rolled over, limbs flailing disjointedly, his back a mass of blood. Incredibly, he was not yet dead; he began to drag himself forward, his face contorted in agony.

Vogel fired again, a two second burst that ripped through Randall's chest and shoulders. Randall screamed once and then slumped forward for the last time.

Paul only spared him a brief glance; he fired another short burst and then sprinted across the next gap, diving full length into cover, just as Vogel fired again. Paul sat with his back to the wall and checked the ammunition clip on the Sten. There were only about fifteen rounds left; not very much, but it would have to suffice. He reached inside the battledress and took out his Walther automatic, blessing the fact that Randall had not had time to search him. He checked the clip and then stuffed it into his belt.

Right, Vogel, he thought as he estimated the distance to the next cover. It's just you and me, the way it should be.

Tyler found Cummings at the gap in the fence. They could hear the gunfire from within the ruins. "Where are they?" he asked.

"In there somewhere. Randall and the German went in after the killer. There are so many echoes around, it's difficult to tell where they are."

"Did Paul really save the King's life?" Tyler had been given a garbled version of what had happened on the station platform.

"He did. Beautiful rugby tackle, it was."

Tyler shook his head, slowly. "Come on, then. Let's go look for them."

Paul moved rapidly through the ruins, eyes darting restlessly to each side, ready to dive for cover should the need arise. He was fairly certain, however, that Vogel would not be waiting in ambush; he would be making a run for it before any reinforcements arrived.

171

Paul caught sight of Vogel about seventy yards ahead, scrambling over a pile of rubble. Paul dropped behind the remains of a wall just before Vogel reached the top of the pile and Paul watched his quarry through a crack in the wall. As he expected, Vogel paused at the top of the pile to turn round. He gave a brief scan behind him, checking on any pursuit and then jumped down out of sight.

He had evidently not seen Paul, who now broke from cover, sprinting towards the rubble. He scrambled up the slope, falling flat just before he reached the top to peer cautiously over.

There was no sign of Vogel, although there were plenty of places where he could be hiding. Paul strained his ears, listening for any sound. Nothing. Vogel had taken cover; he knew Paul was there and was lying in wait . . . .

Almost too late, Paul realised the trap he had walked into. Vogel was not ahead of him at all. He had circled round and back, outflanking Paul, and was probably moving silently into a position where he would have a clear shot.

Paul reacted immediately. He rose to his feet and launched himself over the summit of the rubble just as Vogel opened fire, off to Paul's right. Paul rolled down the far side, firing off a brief burst in Vogel's direction and then scambled into cover.

He peered cautiously around the corner and was rewarded by a burst of fire from behind a low ruined wall about thirty yards away. He evaluated the situation rapidly; he reckoned he had enough ammunition for one short burst but no more than that. There were no choices left. He did not have enough ammunition for a prolonged gun battle; he had to finish it now.

He looked around quickly and picked up a rock that was about the size and shape of a grenade. He hefted it carefully, testing its weight, and then lobbed it into the air in a high, curving arc that would bring it down just behind Vogel; with any luck, it would distract him just long enough to enable Paul to break cover without being cut down.

He waited until he heard the rock land and then leaped over the wall, Sten at the hip. He squeezed the trigger and raked

Vogel's cover, forcing him to keep his head down as he charged straight at him.

Paul hurtled over the wall, dropped the now empty Sten in mid air and pulled the automatic out of his waistband. He landed and rolled smoothly, bringing the gun up ready to fire.

Vogel spun round, reacting very quickly. Paul fired once as he lay on his stomach; the bullet took Vogel in the right shoulder, throwing him backwards. The Schmeisser clattered to the ground. Immediately, Vogel reached out for it with his left hand but Paul sprang to his feet, took three rapid steps and kicked the machine-pistol away.

Vogel rolled over, his left hand reaching inside his jacket. He pulled out a Mauser pistol and loosed off a quick shot, but Paul was already moving off to one side, firing his own gun.

The sounds of the two shots were indistinguishable. Paul staggered back, wincing, as the bullet tore into his left thigh; Vogel also fell back as Paul's shot slammed into his left arm, smashing the elbow. The Mauser fell from his nerveless fingers.

Vogel stared at Paul, awe-struck for perhaps the first time in his life. The man ought to be writhing in agony from that leg wound, yet he was still on his feet, the gun held steady on Vogel's chest. What in hell's name was driving him?

He forced himself to relax and to speak calmly; his only chance now was to take Paul by surprise. "They certainly paid me a compliment sending you after me, Koenig,"

"You know who I am, then?"

"Of course. I recognised you in the girl's flat. The Abwehr sent you to stop me of course."

"Of course."

Vogel laughed softly, despite the pain. "Marvellous. Now we're fighting amongst ourselves. But why did you come after me? You'd done your part. You saved Faust. Why risk your life to come after me?"

"Ilse Lehmann. Does the name mean anything to you?"

Vogel frowned momentarily, then shook his head. "I have never heard of her."

"Two years ago. She was arrested by the Gestapo. You interrogated her, on Heydrich's orders. Right?"

"You seem to know all the facts."

"The trouble was that your lord and master was in too much of a hurry, wasn't he? He wanted quick results, didn't he? What did you use, Vogel? Electric shocks? Or systematic gang-rape? Or were you more subtle and used drugs? No, they wouldn't be quick enough, would they?

"So what happened, Vogel? Wouldn't she talk? Was that it? So you killed her." Paul's voice was icy.

Vogel let his right hand, which had been clutching his shattered left elbow, drop to the ground. "Why was she so special to you? Your girlfriend?"

"More than just that."

"How did you find all this out?"

"I was shown a copy of the record of her interrogation. Your name was at the bottom."

Vogel nodded. "An incentive, or course. They used you, can't you see? Such documents are easily faked. They lied to you, to get you to come after me. I know nothing at all about any girl named Ilse Lehmann and I have never interrogated anybody on Heydrich's orders, or on anyone else's, either. For God's sake, Koenig, I'm an undercover agent, not an interrogator!"

Paul stared at Vogel. Was he telling the truth? Had Canaris deceived him? It was entirely possible; and he had been so consumed by the desire for revenge that he had never questioned the evidence. Until now . . . "You're lying, Vogel. You killed her!"

"As I said, they lied to you. They set you up for this, you—"

Vogel's right hand moved without warning, hurling a shower of small stones and dust at Paul, who instinctively stepped back onto his wounded leg. With a cry of agony, Paul fell backwards as Vogel leaped to his feet and rushed at him. Paul was still toppling backwards as he squeezed the trigger. The bullet slammed into Vogel's chest, stopping him in his tracks. He looked down at the growing stain of red on his chest with an expression of incredulity; it had finally happened to him. He was going to die and there was nothing he could do about it.

He looked at Paul again, now lying on the ground, saw the gun pointing at him . . .

Paul fired for the last time. Vogel spun round, arms outflung, and fell heavily forwards. He was vaguely aware of the stones against his face but he was powerless to move. His last thought was of Maureen and her expression as he had killed her . . .

Then there was nothing.

Tyler found Paul about five minutes later, sitting with his back to the remnants of a wall, five yards or so from Vogel's body.

"You got him them?" he asked, inadequately.

"Yes". Paul was obviously in great pain; Tyler could see the pool of blood beneath his outstretched leg.

"We owe you a great deal," said Tyler, softly.

"My pleasure," said Paul, forcing a smile.

Tyler tore a strip of material from Vogel's shirt and began to fasten a tourniquet around Paul's leg. "So you're Paul? The one I spoke to on the phone?"

Paul nodded. "How is Anton? Lorenz, I mean?"

"Still alive, although he's been knocked around a bit."

"Understandable. We both knew the risks when we started out."

"Just the two of you?"

Paul nodded. "Just the two of us."

Tyler sat back on his haunches. "Why didn't you get out once you knew we'd got Lorenz?"

"Wanted Vogel. Nearly caught him at the girl's flat." He winced at a sudden stab of pain from his leg.

"Don't worry, we'll have you treated soon." Tyler looked thoughtfully at the wounded man. "You said you wanted Vogel? You wanted to kill him?"

"Yes, I did."

"Why?"

"I had my reasons. They were good ones . . . . or so I thought . . . . I'm not so sure, now."

"Why not?"

"Bastard said he didn't do it . . . . said I was used . . . . maybe I was . . . . probably never know now . . . ." Paul fell silent.

Tyler stood up. "Whatever your reasons, we're damned grateful. You deserve a medal for what you did."

Paul smiled again, tiredly. "Somehow, I don't think I'll get one, though."

The crack of a gunshot sent Tyler spinning round. Ten yards away stood Fenton, rifle in hand. Tyler stared at him for several seconds in baffled incomprehension and then turned back to Paul.

He was still sitting propped up against the wall, but there was a growing stain of blood on his chest. His eyes held Tyler's, trying to pass some last, indefinable message, then they glazed over and Paul slumped tiredly to one side.

Tyler did not need to feel for a pulse to know that Paul was dead, shot through the heart.

"For God's sake, why?" shouted Tyler, looking down at Paul's body. "What the hell are you talking about? He saved the King's life! You saw him, for God's sake!"

Fenton's eyes bored into Tyler's. "It never happened, Tyler. Do you understand? It never happened."

Tyler stared at him. "Just what do you mean, it never happened?"

"I mean that no word of this can ever be made public. Ever. There was no alternative."

"Do you mind telling me what you're on about?"

Fenton suddenly sounded tired. "Some days ago, there was an attempt on Hitler's life. A bomb in a briefcase, according to our sources. Unfortunately, it was unsuccessful."

"So?"

Fenton pointed at Paul's body. "I accept that you were right, Tyler. This man and Lorenz belonged to the Anti-Hitler Group. But the conspiracy is finished. All of them are being rounded up. There's not even the remotest possibility now that there will be a negotiated peace, if there ever was any real chance, anyway. So we want unconditional surrender; nothing less. So he—" he gestured at Paul again, "—becomes a liability."

"Why?"

"Can you imagine what would happen if any news of this ever leaked out after the war? That the Germans came within an ace of killing His Majesty and that, even worse from our point of view, his life was only saved by another German? It would make our demands for unconditional surrender appear callous in the extreme."

"So it's all got to be hushed up," said Tyler, an icy edge to his voice.

"Exactly. It must never be revealed how close Vogel came to success and how he was prevented from carrying out his mission. It would be far too—embarrassing—to His Majesty's Government."

"So, to save—embarrassment," said Tyler, stressing the word, "—he had to die?" He pointed at Paul.

"What else were we to do? How could we trust him to keep silent after the war? There was no alternative."

"Oh, for God's sake! Who would have believed him? Who would have taken his word for it?"

"There would be Lorenz's testimony as well, remember. There would be interested parties who might well, at some future date, use this incident against us if they were to get to know about it. The Russians, for example."

"So he had to die. To keep his mouth shut. And Lorenz?"

"The same, I'm afraid."

Tyler looked down at Paul, remembering his last words before Fenton killed him. He had known, Tyler realised. He had known that he would not be allowed to live and tell his story. "Not much of a reward for a man who saved the King's life," he murmured, half to himself.

Fenton heard him. "I know how you feel, Tyler, but there really was no alternative."

As he heard the phrase "no alternative" again, something seemed to snap inside Tyler. He spun round to face Fenton and brought his knee up into the other man's groin. Fenton screamed and doubled up, clutching at his crushed testicles. Tyler grabbed him by the hair and lifted his head up, smashing his right fist into Fenton's face. Fenton reeled back, his jaw broken.

As suddenly as it had come, Tyler's anger evaporated. He stood looking down at Fenton, who was making little whimpering sounds. He pointed at the body of the man whose real name, he suddenly realised, he did not know.

"That was from him, you little bastard. Not half what you deserve."

He felt suddenly drained, empty. Slowly, he began to walk back towards the station.

EPILOGUE

It was never admitted that the attempt to kill King George VI had occurred by either the British or the German Intelligence Services. The British were understandably reluctant, for exactly the reasons given by Fenton to Tyler, to admit that their monarch had come so close to assassination; still less were they willing to reveal how his life had been saved. The biggest 'cover-up" in the history of British undercover operations was ordered. The crowds standing outside Rochester station were never given any explanation for the explosions and gunshots that they had heard. The King himself convinced them that nothing untoward was happening; he reappeared in the forecourt, less than a minute after being knocked off his feet by a man he had never seen before, and would never see again. He proceeded to walk about, chatting to the local dignitaries and waving to the crowd, behaving as though everything was as it should be. The spectators followed his lead and ignored the explosions and the gunfire; they assumed it was an army exercise. As for the troops involved, every last one of them was made to sign the Official Secrets Act, promising never to reveal what had happened. The few waiting passengers in the station on the day suffered a similar fate. An immediate D-notice was slapped on the whole affair, so that all that appeared in the press was a straight forward account of a royal visit. Clearly, nothing had happened; the King was palpably unharmed and so there was nothing to be concerned about. Finally, all photographs, notes and records of that morning were seized and quietly destroyed. The incident was buried without trace.

On the German side, the SS Hierarchy were as reluctant as the British to admit that anything had happened. Himmler, the head of the SS, and Kaltenbrunner, the head of the Reich Security Service, were both questioned about Vogel's mission after their arrests in 1945; both insisted that they had never heard of it. None of the Anti-Hitler Group who had been involved in Operation 'Faust' were alive by the end of the war; Canaris was executed by the Nazis in April 1945 for his involvement in the Bomb Plot and Anton Lorenz was shot dead while trying to escape, according to the official report, on August 12th, 1944.

Fenton spent several weeks in hospital during August and September, 1944, but then resumed his duties. He was forced to resign in 1951, a victim of the Burgess and Maclean scandal. He went into a quiet retirement, resisting suggestions by his erstwhile colleagues to write his memoirs. He was knocked down and killed by a car outside his home in May, 1953; the driver was never identified. Menzies resigned his post in August, 1944, and returned to his estate in Hampshire. He was killed in a hunting accident in March, 1947, when he was thrown from his horse; his widow couldn't understand it—he had always been such a good horseman.

Tyler, despite misgivings, remained in MI5, eventually transferring to MI6 in 1956. He retired in 1980 after a highly successful career and is now living in the Cotswolds with his wife whom he married in 1952. He has just become a grandfather for the third time. He politely declines to answer any questions about the war, other than to admit, reluctantly, that he was involved in the St. Nazaire raid.

Caroline Marriott waited in vain for Paul Keen to write or to come back to her. She eventually married in 1948, calling her only child Paul; nobody really knew why. Her parents had long since forgotten their enigmatic lodger of 1944 but Caroline never did. The marriage was not a success and ended in divorce in 1959. She emigrated to Canada, taking Paul with her. She is now living in Vancouver and her son is a successful architect.

The day after the attempt on his life, King George asked if he could meet Private Paul Keen; he felt he had not had time to thank him sufficiently the day before. Strangely, nobody seemed to know who he was talking about; certainly, the mysterious Private Keen was never found.

And, on a rainy morning in August, 1944, Tyler attended a brief funeral in a small North London cemetery, where a man whose real name he would never know, but who had saved the life of King George the Sixth, was buried in an unmarked grave.